SKETCHY CHARMS

MYSTIC'S END MYSTERIES BOOK 3

LEANNE LEEDS

BADCHEN PUBLISHING

Sketchy Charms
Published by Badchen Publishing
4500 Williams Dr., Suite 212-269
Georgetown, TX 78633 USA

SKETCHY CHARMS

ONE

"There are no rules in art," I told the group of elderly residents sitting before their canvases. "If you want to paint with your fingers, *do* so. If you prefer to paint with oils, do so. Stick figures, polka dots, complementary or clashing colors...the charm of art is that it's *uniquely* you. Rules only apply to you if you accept them as limitations on your creativity."

"Heh, I bet Chief Clutterbuck would agree with you on his *own* behalf, but not on *any* of ours." Harold Whatnow, a frail elderly gentleman with a shock of silvery hair standing straight up, chuckled to himself as his gloved hand smeared purple oil pigment on his canvas.

"What now?" Josephine Roberts cackled, elbowing Miss Bessie and nodding, impressed with the play on words.

The portly Miss Bessie rolled her eyes at her friend. Harold frowned.

"The Whatnow family name has a *proud history* in this town, woman. That there joke may have been amusing the *first* time I heard it," Harold barked at her as he swiveled in his chair. "But you're about sixty years too late to get a laugh out of me!"

"No one gets a laugh out of you, Harold," Vito Salvatore called raspingly across the room, peppering his canvas with black polka dots. The thick-bodied man squinted at each dot through his dense glasses, nodding to himself before he proceeded. "You're an old curmudgeon determined to suck the *last* ounce of joy out of our remaining days. And let's face it, we don't *have* all that many days remaining. Though hopefully I have at least one more than you."

"What are you going on about now, Vito?"

"The last thing I want to hear about is that corrupt Clutterbuck fella," Vito grumbled more to himself than Harold. "Inept *idiot*."

"Inept enough that you get to live here going to a craft class instead of up the road in the gray bar hotel where you belong, you *fakaloo artist!*" Harold hollered. He attempted to force himself out of his wheelchair to confront Vito.

"Sit down, palooka, before I get up and *make* you sit down," Vito warned him. He peered past his canvas and narrowed his eyes. "Well, in five minutes, since that's how long it'll take you to get your old bones upright."

"Okay, gentlemen, let's cut it out and focus on our canvases, shall we? The art show is in just two days," I told the room with a glance of irritation. "If you want these works on display, they have to be finished today."

There were two groups of students that could be a challenge to teach. Toddlers and the elderly. Toddlers because they were still *learning* how to behave, and the elderly because they understood they didn't have to behave anymore.

"If you two give Fortuna a hassle, she won't come back, and we'll lose art class, you nitwits." Karen Aston glared at both of the men. "And we haven't got to the pottery! I want to make a container for my daughter. So sit, you two, and *behave!*"

"I'm sitting," Vito told her. "*Been* sitting, Karen."

"All right, all right, Karen, don't get your

bloomers in a twist," Harold told her, falling back into his wheelchair with a thud.

"Fortuna? Fortuna?" Jessica Ambrose, a mild, sweet septuagenarian, waved her hand from the other side of Miss Bessie. "I dropped my fan brush on the floor," she pointed to the brush next to her, looking flustered. It was just out of reach.

"No problem, Jess, I'll just get this one into the sink and grab you another one." I gave her a new fan brush and picked up the discarded one off the floor. "Everyone has about fifteen minutes until I have to go, so if you have questions, let me know."

"*I* have two questions," Vito called when I turned around from the sink. "Are you single, Fortuna? And how do you feel about older men?" He wiggled his bushy eyebrows at me. They traveled an impressive distance across his wrinkly forehead.

"You ask her that question every time," Miss Bessie complained.

"That's only because I *never* get the answer I'm looking for," Vito told Miss Bessie, then winked at me.

"You have enough women, Mr. Salvatore." Rick Taylor, a linebacker-built nurse, walked into the room and handed a little cup to Vito. The old man downed the pills in one gulp and waved away the water the nurse provided.

"You're just jealous that I don't leave any for you," Vito responded to Rick with another good-natured wink in my direction.

"You don't leave any for *anybody*," Harold murmured.

"What was that, Harold?" Vito called.

"Nothin', nothin'," the cantankerous old man informed him.

* * *

Vito Salvatore's question troubled me. Not that the old man's flirtation offended me—he was more friendly than he was lecherous. His question did, however, remind me it had been *two months* since I'd seen, heard from, or talked to Martin Salvi.

"Can I help?" Rick joined me at the industrial-sized sink. The six art class inhabitants of Mystic Memories Senior Living, jokingly called *Wrinkle City* by Mystic's End residents, had been escorted into the dining area for lunch, and I was just tidying up from the weekly art class I volunteered to teach.

"Sure. If you want to collapse the easels and put them back in the art closet, that'd be great."

"You got it," he said, and he cleared out the various art supplies from the multipurpose room. "If you're hungry, by the way, the food today is somewhat edible. Well, it's not *completely* inedible. You're welcome to a plate, as always."

"I'm meeting Pepper for lunch in about fifteen minutes at the diner. Thanks, though," I explained to him with a grin.

He grinned back and quietly returned to his work.

Rick's rather benign invitation made my stomach grumble, and I wistfully recalled the gourmet meals that Martin used to bring me.

That is, when he was still *talking* to me.

Which now he was *not*.

"Oh, I almost forgot!" Rick dashed over to the employee lockers tucked into a corner of the room. With a quick whirling of the lock, he tugged and pulled out a shoebox. "When I was out this past weekend, I found a lot of tiny crystals. Too small to sell, but I thought you might use them for some art project."

"Crystals?"

"No one's told you about the Arkansas crystals?" Rick asked, astonished. He laid the shoebox down and opened it up. Rick had filled the box with small, glittering rocks. "Those are rock crystal, smoky quartz. There are even a few amethysts in there, and jasper."

"These are beautiful, Rick," I breathed. I held one up to the light. "You mined these yourself?"

"It's a hobby," he shrugged, nodding. "I like to go out on weekends and see what I can find. There's even a state park with a diamond mine—it's the only diamond-bearing site in the entire world that anyone can just walk into and start digging."

"Really?"

"Well, clearly, there's an entrance fee," Rick laughed. "Sure, the chances of finding a huge diamond are, like, one in a billion or something. But what's life without faith, right?"

"Well, good luck on your diamond hunt." I turned an amethyst back and forth.

"I only do the diamond thing once a month," Rick told me. I handed him back the lavender-colored crystal. "Usually I just go into the woodlands around town, near the river and stream beds, in the Ouachitas. There are lots of deposits around here that people know about," he told me, and suddenly dropped his voice. "And some that people don't."

"Well, that's not secretive at all," I laughed.

"It's really serious," he smiled and inclined his head. "Well, maybe not *extremely* serious. But more serious than you would think for a bunch of people rushing around searching for sparkly things in the mud. If you ever want to go out and dig, let me know. I've got extra tools."

I was immediately on guard, not sure whether

Rick was presenting a cordial invitation, or hitting on me in a more casual way than I was used to (considering Martin's over-the-top wooing of me). "I'll think about it, but my shop's open on the weekends, so it *might* be hard to get away."

"Right, right," Rick nodded, his voice faintly disappointed. "Well, in any case, I hope you can use them."

"Absolutely," I strode across the room and placed the shoebox in the supply closet. "I'm sure the folks would love to use them in something. Thanks for thinking of them, Rick."

"Of course," he beamed at me, leaving no ambiguity that it *wasn't* the Wrinkle City art class artists he'd been thinking of.

* * *

"Stop it," Pepper told me as I gazed off distractedly while picking at my chopped salad. The two of us were sitting in the back corner at the Mystic Diner while she flipped through the musical selections of the tabletop jukebox. "If you don't quit moping, I *will* play 'Bye Bye Love' by The Everly Brothers just to get the *proper* mopey ambiance."

"I'm not moping," I told her distractedly. "I don't mope."

"You may think you don't mope." Pepper narrowed her eyes. Scanning me up and down, she rolled her eyes. "But you do. You look *straight-up super-mopey*. It's been two months already. Let it go. He's not worth it, and sulking *doesn't* suit you."

As blunt as she was being (and, to be honest, when *wasn't* she blunt?), Pepper was right. Well, not about him not being worth it. Martin Salvi, the handsome operations manager of the Mystic's End Entertainment Complex, hadn't spoken to me in two months. He hadn't said goodbye, he *hadn't* explained his absence...well, not to me.

Detective Gabriel Wilcox, Pepper's ex and Miss Bessie's grandson, had exploded in an *outstanding* display of outrage after Pepper and I got ourselves—and his grandmother, Miss Bessie —*accidentally* held at gunpoint by a murderer. He insisted he was done with Pepper and me, that we took too many risks. He said Martin felt the same way.

Which, you know, was an *absurd* overreaction. Everything was *fine*. No one got shot. Bad guys went to the prison on the hill. On the whole, it was a successful intervention if I say so myself.

And it wasn't like I had a *choice*, really, after the police department tried to pin a *murder* on me.

But...you wouldn't know everything worked out by how long Gabe was hanging on to his anger over our having gotten into that position. Or by Martin dropping our friendship like a hot potato just as it looked like it would turn into something more.

"Have you talked to Gabe?" I asked Pepper.

"For the tenth or hundredth or *thousandth* time, no, I have not talked to Gabe," Pepper took a vulgar, loud, slurpy draw from her chocolate milkshake. "I haven't talked to Gabe, *you* haven't talked to Martin, they both think we're more trouble than we're worth, and we should wash our hands of them. I have. Why can't you?"

"I don't enjoy being cut out of someone's life with no explanation," I told her. I continued to move the lettuce around on the plate. "The friendship between Martin and me didn't end, it just *disappeared*," I told her. Lowering my voice to a whisper, I continued, "Do you have *any* idea what it's like for a telepath not to know what someone thinks or feels about something so—"

"Probably the same as it feels when I can smell a fact but can't put my hands on it. It drives me nuts."

"Exactly!"

"But that's your own fault," Pepper told me, and then popped a french fry in her mouth. Pointing her salty finger at me, she looked me in the eye. "You can find whatever it is you want to know in his head, and you cleave to your silly moral compass thing—"

"Silly moral comp—"

"Yes, your silly moral compass! You could know, get some closure on it, and move on. But you don't—so, I have no sympathy for you. You could end your own misery with a twirl of your fidget fingers."

"Don't be so melodramatic. I'm *not* miserable," I told her absently.

"If you push around that salad any longer without swallowing any of it, the lettuce will wither. Just like your love life."

"Shut up, Pepper."

"Get over it, Fortuna."

"How do you feel about being a toad?" I shot back as I hoisted my hand.

"Better than I would feel about being some miserable woman who can't get over a man that treated her like she was disposable," Pepper shot back.

I glowered at Pepper and struggled to quell the impulse I had to zap her into the nether realms, but as our eyes locked across the table, I could read her worry for me.

And her outrage at Martin over what he'd done to me.

I realized she was coming from a place of

concern, and a place of guilt—it *was* Pepper who pushed me into delving into the murder case that almost got us killed. I let out a bitter sigh and hurled down my fork.

"Look, I don't want to fight—"

"We *weren't* fighting," Pepper replied, her tone gentler than it had been. "If I *ever* pick a fight with you, trust me, you'll know it."

"I just want to know why he did it. That's it. But," I explained again, running my hand through my hair, "I don't want to go crawling back to him pleading for an explanation. That's just humiliating, and I don't deserve it. I don't want to be another Evangeline Laroux in his harem of dropped women."

"Oh, galloping gremlins, Fortuna—you could *never* be Evangeline Laroux!" Pepper replied, horrified at the thought of me being anything like the sultry bottle-blonde who raced after Martin with the same persistence as a bloodhound hot on a trail. "That woman...Fortuna, no. You're *not* her. That's not this. You guys were getting tight, and suddenly he withdrew. That would upset *anyone*."

"Yeah, I guess," I told her, shrugging.

"Look, I'm not saying you're wrong for feeling how you do." Pepper leaned her chocolate shake toward me and offered me a sip. "I'm just saying that you've fretted over the guy almost as long as you guys were friends. It's time to move on."

I nodded and sipped the chocolate shake.

Not like there was anyone I needed to watch my figure for.

TWO

My Wrinkle City art class had dressed up for their art exhibit.

Well, everybody *except* Harold, who showed up wearing a stained button-down shirt and a grimace.

Miss Bessie and Josie Roberts lightly pushed Jessica Ambrose's mechanical wheelchair. All three women wore ankle-length gowns, simple but elegant jewelry, and their makeup looked professionally done. When Liz, my next-door neighbor, and owner of Mystic Cuts, darted out from behind them, I understood the home must have called her in to doll up the aged women. They looked ecstatic.

"Hey, you have someplace I can lock up my makeup bag?" Liz held up an enormous leather box with a handle on it. I waved her over to the art supply cabinet, now concealed behind large mobile panels. "Thanks," she said, locking the door. "This is a neat shindig."

I peered around and had to admit Liz was right.

Rick had signed up to be in charge of preparing the room, and he had gone above and beyond for the small fundraiser. Spotlights shone on the residents' handiwork, non-alcoholic champagne in plastic flutes blanketed a counter along one side of the room. *Mr. Rice Guy* had contributed an assortment of delicate little canapés and hors d'oeuvres for attendees to snack on. The rented mobile panels lined up around the perimeter hid the institutional look of the room, and for this evening, at least, the place appeared to be a small art gallery.

"They really outdid themselves," I responded, straightening one of Harold's landscapes.

"Well, so did you, Fortuna." Liz gestured to me. "None of this would happen if it weren't for you. I have to confess, those ladies were *giddy* while I worked on their hair and makeup. You'd assume they were going to a magnificent ball."

"I'm so glad," I laughed and then frowned as I looked at the women. "Wait, where's Karen?"

"My makeup was *not* high-end enough to touch her face." Liz rolled her eyes. "I swear that woman hasn't softened as she matured. She's petrified, like wood."

Vito and Karen walked in together. Both gasped at the metamorphosis of the area.

"My goodness, it looks like an authentic art show!" Karen exclaimed, gaping. "Here, at Mystic Memories! I would not have believed it if you *told* me this was how it would look."

"I explained how it would look, Karen," Rick Taylor replied. He and another employee rolled in a small ice machine and placed it in the corner. "You asked me *at least* fifty times, and I told you. Every time."

"Don't be unkind, young man," Karen huffed, her cheeks turning crimson with embarrassment or annoyance, I couldn't tell which. "You told me what it would look like. I just didn't *believe* you."

"Yes, ma'am," Rick said, a smile hovering on his lips, while he plugged in the machine. He caught my eye and winked. I smiled back.

"Okay, everyone, gather around, please," I announced. I left Liz on the side of the room and strode into the center. The art class six shuffled, rolled and strolled up to me.

It took two minutes.

I waited.

Once they were close enough to form a circle, I spoke again. "First, I want to congratulate you all on the work that you've done. These pieces are lovely."

And they were. Some of my most senior students had a true creative flair.

"Who's the *best*, do you think?" Karen asked me shrewdly.

"Fortuna is, for coming here and setting up this program," Rick called as he brought in chairs from outside the room.

Liz lifted her eyebrow, casting a knowing glance at me. I hurriedly shifted my gaze to fend off her implied question.

"The true winners are Mystic's End Greyhound Rescue. All the proceeds from the sale of your art will go to supporting the retired racers that come off the track," I said as Gideon, my greyhound, slithered out from under the refreshment stand and wagged his tail.

Then he shot a vision into my head of a miniature hot dog.

I stared at him and shook my head no.

He whimpered and wandered away, snout to the floor, searching for discarded food.

"Now, just because this is a fundraiser doesn't mean you should look upon it as any less than you would a legitimate art show—because *it is*. Hang out in front of your panel, talk to people about your art, your influences. People buy art they have a relationship with," I told the six looking at me attentively. "Help them make that connection with your piece. With *you*."

They all nodded.

"Okay, folks, let's get settled in for the evening, and good luck," I called out cheerfully. Gideon barked.

"I can't believe they let her bring a *dog* in here," Karen said as Vito helped her to her art panel.

"We're raising money for the dogs! Why wouldn't you want a greyhound in here if we're raising money for greyhounds, Karen?" Miss Bessie called while she limped toward her panel.

"I'm fine raising cash for them, but I shouldn't have to *see* them!" Karen snapped back.

Gideon sneezed.

* * *

I remained off to the side and out of the way, preferring to give the artisans their night to shine. Since the fundraiser was at a senior care center, I didn't expect the town to show up in force, but at least fifty people arrived to meander around the hall. Though there were many family members of the artists, there were at least forty that only came for the event.

"Okay, I got pictures of everybody." Pepper came back over to Liz and me. "Got everyone's narrative, or at least enough to scribble up something that won't be a *total* puff piece."

"How do you go from writing an exposé on the murder of Hugh Maddox to a writeup of a tiny fundraiser at an old folks' home?" Liz asked her, bewildered.

"Just lucky, I guess." Pepper crammed her camera back in her satchel. Looking up toward the door, she glowered. "Oh, great. "I have another two months of sulking to look forward to now." Abruptly, her tone became sharper. "What the...are you *kidding* me?"

I glanced toward the door to see Martin Salvi, the man who dropped me off after I was *practically shot* and never talked to me again, looking through the room. Our eyes met momentarily, and he shifted his gaze away instantly. Standing beside him as if they showed up together was...Gabriel Wilcox.

"Wait, they're buddies now?" Liz asked, dumbfounded. "I thought they couldn't stand each other?"

"They can't. At least, I *think* they can't. They must have just entered at the same time," I responded. Claire, Miss Bessie's caretaker, walked in behind them.

Pepper frantically waved her over.

"Hi, everyone," Claire said merrily. "Fortuna, this is—"

"Yeah, yeah, it's great," Pepper said, cutting her off. "Did you see whether Martin and Gabe arrived together?"

"They got out of Martin's limo," the shy Claire responded softly, panic overtaking her face as Pepper seemed prepared to interrogate her right there next to the pigs in a blanket. "Why?"

The journalist's voice hardened when she saw Martin and Gabe part ways in the sea of people. "What are they up to?"

"I don't know, I—"

"I wasn't asking you," Pepper shot back. Claire bit her lip, but looked relieved. "It was a rhetorical question."

"Stop snapping at Claire, it's not her fault," I told Pepper. Her nose practically twitched on her face. "Smelling a fact you can't quite put your hands on?" I slipped her an amused glance.

"Yeah, I wonder—" Pepper caught my remark, and her eyes narrowed. "Oh, I get it. Ha ha. Hilarious. This differs from moping about some boy. This isn't about a heartbreak. They're up to something."

"Norman Mailer said obsession is the single most wasteful human activity, you know," I told her, crossing my arms.

"Obsession makes *everything* possible," Pepper replied. "Novala Takemoto."

"Who's that?" Liz asked, mystified.

"You have a phone, look it up," Pepper told her. "Speaking of..." Pepper pulled her phone out and her thumbs flew over the screen. At the sound of a bell somewhere in the room, she looked up and peered at Gabe.

Gabriel Wilcox, standing next to Miss Bessie, coolly removed his phone from his pocket and checked the screen. His shoulders fell slightly at reading Pepper's message, and then he slowly typed back without ever looking at her.

Pepper looked at the screen as if she could will the three tantalizing dots to turn into words. Finally, her phone made a soft beep, and she cursed under her breath.

"What?" I asked her. She handed me the phone.

Why are you here with Martin? When did the two of you become friends? You swore you thought he was corrupt, what's changed?

His response?

Must frustrate you not to know things about people you care about.

"Well, *that* was snide," I passed the phone back to her.

"I can't believe he's treating me like this."

"So, I mean, you *did* almost get his grandma, the woman that raised him, killed, Pepper," Claire said hesitantly.

"Actually, Fortuna had a bigger role in that one than I did," Pepper responded, her eyes fastened to the back of Gabe's head as if she could will him to turn and acknowledge her.

"Thanks!" I frowned.

Pepper shrugged without glancing at me.

"Look, I see Gabriel quite a bit," Claire said suddenly in a clear voice. We watched Gabriel lean down with his arm around Miss Bessie. "That his grandmother could be killed...well, it brought up unpleasant memories for him." Pepper didn't turn around. "About his mother."

At the mention of the deceased Mary Wilcox, Pepper spun and studied Claire. Her grim face softened as she contemplated the woman's words.

"He *will* get over it, I'm certain of it," Claire told Pepper. "Miss Bessie has told him time and time again these past few months that he's absurd. His treatment of you and Fortuna both has not... pleased her."

"That doesn't explain what on earth Martin is doing here with him," I replied to Claire.

"Martin's here for his great-uncle," Rick's voice answered from behind me.

I spun and looked at him, perplexed. "His great-uncle? Does he live here?" Martin had revealed no family in this town, much less here at the senior home. In fact, I could have sworn he said he was alone here.

"Sure, you're well acquainted with him," Rick nodded in Martin's direction and pointed. "Vito Salvatore. He's in your class."

I turned and gawked in shock.

* * *

"Fortuna!" Vito wheezed later as I wandered by his panel.

There were several people assembled in front complimenting the old man's art. One person was his great-nephew, Martin Salvi.

Stopping short, I struggled to figure out a way to politely keep going without seeming rude. Then I realized the very fact that I'd paused when he called *probably* meant Vito knew I had heard him, and I didn't want to hurt the old man's feelings. It wasn't his fault his nephew was a big jerk.

Sighing, I turned around and walked over.

"Hi, Vito, how are you enjoying the show?" I

asked him, my voice ringing with cheer and friendliness.

Vito gave me an odd look. Probably because my voice rarely rang with cheer or friendliness.

And certainly not both at once.

"I wanted to introduce you to my nephew, Martin." Vito turned to his nephew. Martin towered over the short old man, but both had the same build—muscled and thick, like rugby players. "Martin, this is the art teacher I was tellin' you about. She made all this possible."

"Fortuna and I have been previously acquainted, Uncle Vito," Martin told his uncle in a honeyed voice. "She purchased the greyhound that's winding his way through the crowd in an attempt to get as many of the tiny hot dogs as he can."

He didn't mention we had spent time together so much as once, never mind that we'd done it week after week for several months. Or that he had repeatedly asked me to go out on a date.

Previously acquainted.

"You *bought* the dog?" Vito asked me, surprised. "Not adopted?"

I nodded. "I wasn't really looking for a pet at the time," I told Vito. "Gideon kind of found me, and I got pretty attached to him. The only way to keep him was to purchase him from Dexter Kane, so I did."

For fifty-thousand dollars, but no need to mention that.

"Sounds like you *stick*," Vito nodded approvingly and patted me on the shoulder. Martin frowned and gazed off toward the champagne table. "That's good. Loyalty is *good*."

"I'm not sure I follow," I told him, confused.

"Our family, we value loyalty," Vito told me, his eyes darting to Martin briefly before settling back to meet mine. "When we care about someone, we *stick*. Loyal to the core, we are. We don't cut and run. Right, Martin?"

"Excuse me, I'm going to get a glass of that champagne," Martin told his uncle without looking at me. He spun on his heel and walked toward the other side of the room as fast as he could go without making a scene.

I blinked back tears. I was surprised at how much it hurt for Martin to physically turn his back on me and race away.

Vito sighed. "There now, *none* of that. I can't stand to see a pretty girl cry," Vito told me quietly, a muscle in his jaw twitching as he gazed after his nephew. "I'm sorry my nephew is being such a dolt. You have to understand, Fortuna, he's not used to...

well, let's just say the world he came from has *different* rules."

I wiped my eyes quickly to hide the tears and stared at Vito. Did he know who I was? What happened between Martin and me? Why had he never said anything?

"You have questions," Vito guessed. I nodded. "I wish I could tell you I got answers for you, but they ain't mine to give, you know?"

"I don't, Vito, to tell you the truth," I told him. "Did Martin tell you about our relationship?"

"That it was you?" Vito asked. "No, but we don't name names in our family," he told me mysteriously. "Safer that way for everybody. He told me about you, though. I put two and two together a while back, realized you were the art lady he'd fallen hard for."

"This is a small town, it's not like you'd need a name to figure out it was me, I guess," I pointed out.

"Yeah, well," Vito sighed. "I think Martin realized that, too. But I think he'll come back to you."

I blinked and stood straight up, tense, Pepper's words from the diner playing in my mind. "Back?"

"Eventually."

"I don't *want* him *back*," I told Vito so vehemently the old man backed up a step. "Sorry. I mean, maybe a part of me does," I admitted, lowering my voice. "But he left with *no* explanation, *no* word, and just stopped returning my phone calls. How could I ever trust him again? I don't want him back. I just want to know *why* he did what he did."

"See, that's what happens when people don't stick," Vito sighed gruffly, shaking his head. "Trust. Loyalty. If you don't have that with the people you care about, the whole thing? The *whole* thing goes bad."

"I...um...sure," I agreed, even though I didn't know what, exactly, I was agreeing to.

"I'll talk to him," Uncle Vito said with a nod to himself. "If someone had done to me what he did to you?" Uncle Vito whistled and shook his head. "My Dora would have taken a mallet to my head if I pulled this on her. A mallet, I tell ya. And *not* the bouncy rubber kind you use just for making a point. Whack, right between the eyes." His eyes softened. "She was a good egg, my girl."

"I'm so sorry for your loss," I said automatically, but sincerely.

"You're a good egg, too, Fortuna." Vito reached out and gave me a brief hug. He smelled like an expensive musky cologne, a fragrance that reminded me of Martin. "I'm sorry my nephew came with baggage. You give old Uncle Vito some time. *I'll* unpack those bags."

When he pulled back, he reached down and

scratched Gideon's head. I hadn't even realized the dog had come up to stand beside me.

"It's fine, Vito—"

"You call me Uncle Vito, girly." I blushed.

"Uncle Vito, I—"

"Now be a good girl and go mingle," he said as his eyes searched the crowd. "I need to talk some sense into my nephew, and that coward won't come back here while you're here."

THREE

"The entire night? He didn't talk to you *at all*?" Liz asked me the morning after the art show, her eyes wide with dismay.

"Well, if we were near each other, which happened only briefly, he was courteous to me." We were perched on stools behind the counter of my shop drinking cappuccino.

It was just before ten, and Liz had rushed in to get the lowdown on the preceding night so she could compare my story to the one being told by her hairdressing clients that day. "Uncle Vito 'introduced' us, Martin made pleasantries, and suddenly got *very* interested in the wine bar."

"I don't know how you put up with something

like that, truly, Fortuna," Liz shook her head and took another sip of cappuccino.

"What am I supposed to do about it?"

"She *doesn't* put up with it," Spike said, gazing out the front window onto the sunny street to observe the mid-morning walkers as they strode in rhythm along the pavement. "He didn't give her a chance to put up with it. *I* put up with it, though. *Two months* now."

"You realize she can't hear you." I glared at the complaining punk ghost. I hadn't complained to my spectral roommate all *that* much.

Gideon barked.

"Spike?" Liz guessed.

"He says I don't put up with it," I told her, and described the rest of his remark.

"You know, she puts up with *you*, buddy," Liz called loudly. She lifted her chin toward the room and her eyes hunted for the specter she couldn't see. "*I* recall working with you, Spike," Liz told him, alluding to their time together as teens working here back when it was a record store. "Putting up with you can be no minor feat sometimes."

"I guess you're not very *busy* anymore, Liz, since you can sit around our shop and *blab* all day," Spike jeered at her. "Just my luck that I get to listen to you in the afterlife, too."

"I'm not translating sarcastic comebacks," I announced to the ghost.

Liz's face twitched with curiosity.

"Ugh! I wish I had some way to communicate," Spike complained. He sat down on the couch. "This drives me nuts sometimes."

"Actually, there's an app for that," I told Spike.

"What do you mean?" Spike looked bewildered.

"An app for what?" Liz asked me.

"I downloaded it the other day. Well, one of them," I picked up my phone and opened the *Ghosts, Ghosts Everywhere* app that alleges it can scan for ghosts in the immediate area—and allow them to "talk."

"I presume it's supposed to be like a modern Ouija board or something. I do not follow how what you say is supposed to come up on the screen, but it *claims* it can do that."

"It also claims it's for entertainment only." Liz snatched my phone and studied the flashing dots on the application.

"Yeah, well, it was free, so I thought it might be fun to see if it worked. It is probably bunk, but what the heck, right?" I gestured to Spike. "So? Say something."

"What do you want me to say?" he asked.

"Want. Say," a mechanical voice exploded from

the phone. Gideon wagged his tail furiously and Spike's eyes grew wide.

"Did that thing just repeat what I said?"

"Thing. Said," the app repeated.

"Try talking more slowly," I told him, leaning in close to Liz as we both watched the app. The circle at the top that scanned for ghosts flashed a speck repeatedly. Below the circle, words flashed and the app's computer-generated male voice spoke.

"How...slow...should...I..."

After a pause, the neon green words emerged as the app spoke. "How. Slow. Should. Eye."

"Holy cow, that's *amazing*!" Spike exclaimed with a shriek. The ghost began ping-ponging back and forth around the storefront. Gideon barked joyfully, bouncing after him.

"Cow. Zing," the app related.

"What's a cowzing?" Liz asked, puzzled.

"Well, it's not really any *quicker* than a Ouija board, but I have to admit, I didn't think it would work," I told them both.

Liz grabbed my phone and scanned the app name, dropping it quickly to launch the app store on her own phone. The speaker on my phone continued to pick up odd words as Spike rambled on with excitement.

"I'm turning the sound off." Liz tapped around her screen. "Spike, I'll put the app on vibrate and leave it running so it records your words. Wow," her voice fell and her eyes grew wide. "It's like a text message from the great beyond," she sighed. "That's just *crazy*."

"If the great beyond is Mystic's End, we're *all* in trouble," Spike laughed. Gideon barked again.

"Great. Mystic. Trouble," my app said emphatically.

I frowned.

* * *

"Here." Pepper slapped an old, rolled-up parchment down on the shop counter in front of my bowl of soup. I stared at her and then looked down at the dusty paper.

"Um. Thank you?" I peeked up.

"Don't you want to ask me what it is?" Pepper asked me, peering over her glasses, her lips pursed.

"That's a touchy question if you think about it. I don't know. *You* tell *me*. Do I want to?"

"Before I say anything, is there anybody here?" Pepper looked through the empty room and stomped toward the back to make sure that no one was in the shop.

"Nope. It's the middle of the week, and we haven't started summer art camp yet," I called to her while she searched my empty place of business. "Things might pick up toward the end of the day."

"I'm. Here," the *Ghost* app blared out mechanically.

"What was that?" Pepper demanded.

"This app picks up things Spike says, but...he said nothing," I said pointing at my phone.

The ghost suddenly poofed into view with a flash of sparkles and glow. "That's *incredible!*"

"Incredible," the app repeated.

"How did you do that?" I quizzed him. "I expected if I could hear you, it could, but I didn't. How the heck did it do that?"

"I can kind of teleport around now. It's like I lug around my own personal Star Trek transporter or something," Spike told me proudly. He poofed out of view in front of me and quickly appeared next to the front window. "I can also, like, half-teleport, I guess...like, there's someplace I am and I can hide there in-between but see everything you guys are doing. It's foggy, though. Like, hazy."

"Hazy," the app agreed.

Spike disappeared again.

"You have to be kidding me," my friend said after snatching up my phone and scouring the flashing lights and typed words. "I have to write about this on my blog," she babbled. "It *really* can do what it claims? How does it work? Can it *really* track—"

"Stop. I don't know. It's picking up one ghost, and that's as much as I know. Well, and it's picked up snatches of what Spike's saying, so I can verify that for you," I said.

"Ugh, so many things to look into, so little time," Pepper complained. "You know, before you showed up in Mystic's End, I used to get bored sometimes. Not anymore." She looked between the map and the phone, moaned in frustration, and passed the phone back. "Okay, *map* first."

"Map?"

"This is a sketch of a map." Pepper gently unrolled it. "Mystic's End, the surrounding county. Here," she pointed to a small stream between two larger rivers and touched the parchment. "That's where I expect we'll find your answers."

"Answers to what?"

"What the mystic of Mystic's End *really* is," she replied.

"In the middle of a forest?" I asked her, somewhat doubtful.

"See this?" she asked, pointing to some squiggly lines. I nodded. "I'm almost sure that marks a crystal field full of veins. And this?" She pointed to a lone tree among the squiggles. "This is a tree that marks the area where we'll find it."

"Find *what?*"

"The book." Pepper pulled out an antique, plastic-wrapped library book and shoved it toward me. I glanced at the cover. *The Witch History of Mystic.* "This book says that—"

Pepper stopped speaking abruptly when the bells on the door rang out to indicate a visitor. She scrambled to roll up the map. I glanced around her to discover Uncle Vito strolling in with a glum-looking Martin in tow.

"Idiot," the app rang out mechanically.

* * *

"I wanna get my own paint," Uncle Vito announced as he came up to the counter. "The art show last night made me realize that people really seem to like my stuff. I wanna do it in my spare time. What do ya got for me, Fortuna?"

"I have anything you might need, Uncle Vito," I told him. "We've worked in oils and acrylics already. Did you want to stick with those mediums or try something new?"

Martin remained at the door without joining his uncle.

"Jerk," the automatic voice from my phone said as Pepper tried to snuff out a giggle. I reached over hastily and smashed the buttons until I closed the app, blushing profusely.

"What was that?" Uncle Vito asked amiably. His great-nephew's face remained impassive from his position at the exit.

"A text-to-speech reader," I lied. I slipped my phone beneath the counter and stepped out to meet Uncle Vito. "Mr. Salvi, please have a seat," I told Martin over my shoulder, taking care to keep a formal, distant manner to my voice. "There's complimentary coffee in the—"

"I know where the coffee is, Fortuna," Martin answered quickly without sitting down.

"Blockhead," a female computer voice droned. Pepper held up her phone and waved it at me, grinning mischievously.

"Stop," I whispered forcefully to her. Uncle Vito looked at me, baffled.

Martin seemed like he wasn't taking notice, but I identified the telltale tightening of a tendon in his jaw announcing his discomfort.

With an exhale, Pepper tapped her phone and put it into her pocket, then signaled for me to hurry.

"I think I wanna stick with what I know," Uncle Vito announced loudly, wandering over toward the oils display. "The familiar is *good*. You should never try something different unless you're *sure* the usual no longer works for you, you get my meaning?"

"Uncle Vito, I have a meeting in a half an hour," Martin said from the door with a nervousness I had seldom heard from him. I glanced up and surveyed his face, but it was still stoic—and he refused, as was usual now, to look at me.

"You have fifty years of time ahead of *you*, son," Uncle Vito called to Martin with a half-smile. "My time is much more finite, and that makes it far more important than any meeting you might have, *capisce?*"

Martin rolled his eyes.

"You have some respect for your elders," Uncle Vito warned him.

Martin dropped his head, and then raised his eyes, sighing.

"Sorry, Uncle Vito, it's just a busy day. I'll push it off. You get what you need."

"Good boy. You're never too busy for family. Them's the *rules*," Uncle Vito told him. He randomly grabbed paint colors without paying much attention to what he was grabbing. He flung them all on the counter in a disorganized heap. "Come pay the lady so we can go to lunch. Would you like to come, Fortuna? To lunch I mean?"

Martin froze in mid-step.

"Um, I already have plans with Pepper, Uncle Vito," I lied through my teeth again while gathering up the paints so I could ring them up. "Did you need brushes and a canvas or two?"

"Throw those in there," he agreed, nodding. "The most expensive ones you got, too. Martin can afford it."

Martin had restarted his steps toward the counter, nodding to Pepper as he passed her. She glared back at him and said nothing.

"What do I owe you?" Martin asked pulling out his wallet.

"An explanation," I fired out without thinking as I totaled up Uncle Vito's supplies.

Pepper actually gasped.

I hadn't *intended* to say it out loud.

It just kind of...came out.

I glanced up to see Uncle Vito turning his head away from Martin so my almost-boyfriend (but definitely ex-friend) couldn't observe the old man laughing silently.

"I'm sorry," Martin replied in a strained voice. I peered up, and our eyes met. I couldn't determine whether what he said was a real apology, or a question. I felt a temporary chill caught in Martin's gaze, a silent scrutiny draped in sadness. It blended with something that was almost...fear.

I wanted to feel sorry for him, for the suffering I saw imprinted on his elegant face, the shadows that covered whatever truth I would never learn. I recognized, looking into his eyes, I would never know.

Because he would never tell me.

I wanted to feel bad for him.

But I *didn't*.

"It's two hundred thirty-seven dollars, please," I responded in my best distant shopkeeper voice. As Martin presented his credit card, our fingers touched, and a roar exploded in my mind, a mental blast so intense and so overpowering I thought it would knock me off my feet—

—only to find it quelled when my greyhound, Gideon, pressed affectionately against my leg. I glanced down at him, perplexed, but he merely stared back up at me playfully and wagged his tail.

Weird.

Exhaling, I ran the card, packed up the supplies, and calmly pushed it all across the counter. Martin grabbed both, spun on his heel, and raced out the door. He didn't seem to recognize (or he didn't care) that he left his uncle standing at the counter gazing after him.

Now Vito sighed.

"He's a good boy, Fortuna," Uncle Vito confided softly as he angled toward me. "I know it doesn't seem that way to you, but he is."

"Your great-nephew isn't a child, Mr. Salvatore." Pepper stepped up and stared at the worried old man. He shifted and met her eyes, nodding. "He's not a boy. He's a man—but he certainly didn't *act* like one with Fortuna."

"Things aren't always what they seem, Miss Stanford," Uncle Vito told Pepper. "You, of all people in this town, should know that. Remember that saying, be kind, for everyone you meet is fighting a hard battle?"

"Plato," I nodded.

"No, I think it was Philo of Alexandria," Pepper disagreed.

"It was John Watson," Uncle Vito told us both.

"Sherlock's sidekick?"

"No, the writer Ian Macaroni or Macaroon or something," Uncle Vito explained.

"You just said it was John Watson?" Pepper asked, confused.

"Look, doesn't matter who said it." Uncle Vito waved his hands in the air. "What I'm saying is you don't *know* his battles, Miss Stanford. Yes, I realize he probably doesn't know yours, either, Fortuna," Uncle Vito eyed me up and down. "And what he did was stupid, I admit that. But don't judge him too harshly."

"I can't judge him at all, Uncle Vito," I told the old man. "He hasn't given me an explanation to judge."

The horn of Martin's sports car honked outside.

"I have to go," Uncle Vito said and turned toward the door. "Remember, when he comes to you, listen. Listen with an open mind."

Before I could answer, Uncle Vito was out the door.

"Why is that old man so interested in you and Martin?" Pepper asked me, her eyes narrowing as the old man hopped into the sports car like a man twenty years his junior.

"I don't know, I don't care," I told her, turning back to the map. Gideon continued to press his body against mine and I realized the pressure seemed to make me feel calmer, somehow. I reached down and scratched his head, then turned to Pepper. "Tell me about this tree and book thing."

Pepper glanced out the door and spotted Joe Bradley headed for my front door. With an exasperated sigh, she glared at me. "Your business makes talking about secret stuff incredibly inconvenient. What are you doing tonight? Any evening classes?"

"Last one's at five."

"I'll meet you here at seven. Wear boots." She shoved the map back in her bag. "I'll explain on the way."

"On the way to where?"

"That tree."

FOUR

"Did we have to do this at night?" I asked Pepper as we picked our way through the thick underbrush. The air was cool and clear, still. The stars blinked in the cloudless sky.

"You're open seven days a week, Fortuna," Pepper huffed while pushing a branch out of the way. "Would you have closed shop to go do this? Besides, this way, no one will notice us."

"I'm still recovering from Gideon's purchase decimating my savings, and the town working to shut me down," I told her. An owl hooted. I followed her over what had, at initial glance, looked to be mild hills.

We emerged in a narrow pass. The sweat running down my face and gathering in a multitude of unmentionable places argued against the terrain's gentle appearance. "I need to keep up the momentum I've got. Business is finally going smoothly."

And it was.

There were several classes now full, containing all age ranges, and a few private students that came frequently for supplies. Though I donated my time at Wrinkle City, it looked to have elevated my reputation from possible murderer to a decent, upstanding member of the community.

"Only one momentum you need to concentrate on, and that's our hiking." She darted her light to the west. "I think it's that way."

"You *think?*"

"You know, I'm doing this to help you." Pepper spun and beamed the light directly in my eyes. "You could stop being snarky *two seconds* and maybe, just *maybe*, stop and thank me for doing all the legwork to bring us here."

"You want me to thank you for dragging me into the middle of a forest on a Wednesday night?" I asked her incredulously. "Besides, I'm not being snarky. I showed up, didn't I?"

"I'm doing this to *help* you!" she insisted again, stomping her foot.

"Oh, who are *you* kidding?" I laughed. "You're doing this because you need to know what the mystic thing Miss Bessie did is all about. You're not doing it to help me."

"But it *is* helping you, too!" Pepper exclaimed, her palms wide.

"Sure, that's a side effect, but—"

"Look, little miss *half-a-witch* at *best*, you're the one all wary of everyone in the town," Pepper snapped at me.

I did my best not to laugh. That line, coming from the most tenacious investigative reporter on staff at the Mystic's End Herald, who never met a conspiracy she didn't at least partially accept, was the funniest thing I'd heard all day.

"Pepper, I—"

"I can tell you for a fact—*a fact*—that if some old woman had slapped *me* and granted *me* powers, the first individual I would go talk to about it was *her*. But you? Nope."

"Look, I'm cautious, not suspicious. You're suspicious."

"I'm suspicious of people who *warrant* it, Lucky."

I stared at her. "Lucky?"

"Your name's a damn mouthful," Pepper retorted.

"What the heck is going on with you?" I asked her, narrowing my eyes. Pepper was a little rough around the edges most days, but she was rarely mean. I usually enjoyed her blunt, to-the-point way of speaking.

But this just sounded like she *was* trying to pick a fight.

"Nothing," she muttered, turning away and making her way down the pass. "Nothing. Let's just get this done."

"Pepper, stop," I called out. She snorted and kept trudging. "Pepper Stanford, if you don't stop and tell me what's going on, I *will dig it out of your head myself*!"

The blonde woman whirled on me and planted her feet far apart as if she was preparing for a blow. "You stay *out* of my skull, Fortuna Delphi! I'm *fine*, okay? Just fine!" she huffed. "What do you care, anyway? You're *only* here because I threatened to out you as a witch if you didn't work with me to investigate—"

"Hey!" I said sharply, surprised. This wasn't like Pepper. "Look, I know in the beginning you kind of attached yourself to me because I was a witch and had powers and...Pepper, we're *friends*," I told her softly, moving toward her. "I *care* about you. We're friends. Don't you *know* that?"

She stared at me quietly and then glanced away.

"What is it? Why are you so...so combative

tonight?" As I reached her, I held out my hand, palm up. "Did I do something?"

"I'm just a pain, haven't you heard?" she cracked, crossing her arms. "If you really are my friend, you have terrible—"

"Pepper—"

"Oh, fine," she twisted away and walked to a small boulder that lined the pass. Sitting down, she stared at the ground for a few moments, breathing deeply. Her face was troubled. Finally, she looked up and met my eyes. "I told you Gabriel and I were high school sweethearts, right?"

I nodded.

"Well, we were friends before *that*, even." Pepper peered down at the flashlight. Her fingers played in the beam as she exhaled. "When we were furious at each other, when we broke up all those times...we were still *always* friends." Pepper quickly wiped tears from her eyes. "He's never been *this* mad at me for *this* long. Never. I...I don't know what to do."

"I thought you were okay with it? At the diner, you said—"

She cut me off with a hurt glare. "Some psychic *you* are."

"Oh, Pepper," I sighed.

"And I don't enjoy feeling this way. I feel like a weak-willed idiot, and that's *not* me," she said fiercely straightening her back. "I'm strong. I'm *tough*. I don't care what *anyone* thinks of me. I'm not some wimpy girl that sits in the woods crying over a boy."

"Like me, you mean?" I smirked and walked to stand in front of her.

Pepper looked down and sank deeper into her gloom.

"Yeah, look, I'm sorry about that."

"Sorry about what? Giving me guff for two months over Martin?"

"You weren't allowed to curse much as a kid, were you?" Pepper asked me. I shook my head no. "It shows."

"I barely knew Martin for two months, so I get why you were on me to just get over him leaving," I conceded.

"Ugh, *stop* hovering over me. I feel like you're about to give me detention." I sat down beside her, and she moved a few inches to make room for me on half of the rock.

"I get why you're upset about Martin. I guess I get it because I feel the same way about Gabe—though I didn't want to admit it. When you spoke about getting with Miss Bessie on witch training after the shooting, I figured that would solve the situation with Gabe, at least. I'd be around, he'd mellow. But you didn't."

"I don't want to come between Gabe and his grandmother," I explained to her. "It's not that I don't trust her, or that I don't want to learn from her. Sure, *maybe* it was at first," I shrugged. "Claire was right, though, Pepper—we put Miss Bessie in danger. Gabe has a right to be angry. I wanted to let him work through it first. Granted, I didn't think it would take *this* long, either."

The pale moon was rising in the clear night sky. Pepper and I sat quietly. The star-studded heavens above bathed us in a subdued silvery white as the enveloping forest whispered.

"Yeah, well, he's *not* working through it," she finally admitted. "I appreciate he has a right to be angry. I just can't help but fear this is it for the two of us. I knew we could never be together, but I always counted on the fact that he would be my friend. You know?"

"I know." I put my arm around her. "I'm sorry."

"It's not your fault."

"Yeah, I think it kinda was," I joked, leaning against my crazy partner. "It was my keister in the fire that got us involved with the Maddox murder."

"Okay, so maybe it was. Make it up to me." She pulled away and stood up. "Let's go find that book. Maybe there's a spell in there to fix everything."

* * *

We walked another forty-five minutes quietly, both of us lost in our own thoughts.

Finally, the path led us to a clump of bushes, densely laid. It looked to be almost purposely blocking the very route we were following, like a natural fence.

"This is the way," Pepper said, examining the barrier. "But that thing is *covered* with nettles. We'll require a trip to the emergency room if we try to climb through there."

I frowned, cursing my limited magic repertoire.

"Can you fidget-finger us in?" she asked me.

I examined the facade of sharp branches and inch long thorns. Ten feet tall, the scrub towered over me. Looking right and left, there was no break there, either—the natural wall seemed to go on forever. "I have no idea how to do it. I've mostly learned magic that makes or mends objects. Not destroys them."

"Well, don't *destroy* it. Just make a door," Pepper suggested.

"I don't know how," I told her. "I don't have a door here to duplicate, and to be frank, I think I would just create a door leaning against brambles and branches, anyhow."

"For goodness' sake, Fortuna, you make art *all the time*! Just imagine a freaking tunnel there,"

Pepper pointed with exasperation, "and see if it works!"

I stared at the thicket once more, then closed my eyes.

It wasn't much effort, really, to imagine the brambles in an archway. I opened my eyes and released the vision. A sparkly dust flew toward the bulwark—

—and exploded as it hit.

Then it faded.

The barrier remained impenetrable.

"Well, it was a good idea," I told Pepper. "Maybe we need to come back with some axes?"

"How can we get in...How can we get in..." Pepper paced in front of the grove, biting her lip and squinting at it.

"Come on, forest, that was a *heck* of a hike," I called out to no one in particular. "Let us in, will you? I don't want to have to come back here again."

The ground shuddered.

"What was that?" Pepper stopped pacing, her eyes wide. The shuddering grew strong enough to fling us down into a carpet of fallen leaves. Nothing could have remained standing.

"Earthquake!" I shouted.

I had lived in California.

I knew this feeling.

Or so I thought.

This was beyond *anything* I had encountered before. There was no warning, no lead-up. Just *wham!*

I curled up, face down, my arms protecting my head while the ground beneath me jerked and convulsed. It seemed like I was on a concrete trampoline as the tremors tossed me up and down, up and down. Suddenly, a great and dreadful sound echoed. It was like a baseball bat hitting a ball—but a thousand times louder.

Pepper screamed, but there was nothing I could do to help her. It was all I could do to protect myself as I was tossed like a listing ship in the waves of a hundred-year storm.

Just when I feared the violence would bounce me into a tree, the rumble died down and the surface calmed.

"Are you all right?" I called, scrambling up to my hands and knees. My limbs felt like jello, and I couldn't quite determine whether my stomach had settled back in the place it normally lived.

"Yeah, scraped my knee, but I'm—"

I waited for Pepper to finish her sentence, but there was only silence. "Pepper?" I called out in a panic.

"Yeah, I...I'm here," she responded in a small voice.

"Are you okay?" I demanded, trying to push myself upright.

"I don't know who you are, Fortuna," Pepper continued. "And maybe *you* don't know who you are. But I think...I think...the forest *does*."

I rose up and shifted toward Pepper's voice.

She stood in front of the barrier, now open. Three feet beyond the entrance, a dazzling crystal cluster of vivid blues and greens surrounded a flat slate rock the size of a small boulder. The crystalline points appeared to glow from within, and the surrounding ground looked like someone had turned it over, as if the cluster had been given up by the earth just moments ago.

On top of the slate, a book lay open. Lightning flashed, seemingly generated from within the book itself.

* * *

Once I removed the book from the slate table, it banged shut and the land treated us to another violent upheaval, the earth returning the altar back beneath the ground. The bramble thicket closed, and the woodland was silent.

Pepper and I didn't speak for a while as we walked back. I didn't know what I had just encountered. I was glad it was over, and I was glad neither of us had gotten hurt.

"Have you ever seen anything like that?" Pepper finally asked me, halfway back to the parking lot.

"Like that? No. But I've...I've seen some things. You know, it's funny," I mused, thinking back to the bramble archway. "When Charlotte and Roland made me a witch two years ago? We were in an archway between the two circuses." Pepper and I walked quietly for a few more minutes. "I wonder what it is with magic and archways," I murmured.

"*How* are you so calm?" Pepper asked me, her voice shaky. A raccoon scrambled across the path in front of us and fled into the brush without ever glancing up. "I mean, we just saw something...*miraculous*, Fortuna."

"No more Lucky?" I quizzed her.

"I'm serious." She spun to me, frowning.

"Why are *you* so freaked out? You've talked to ghosts, you know there's a paranormal side to life. What was it about *this* that—"

"Fortuna, you asked the forest to give you something, and the forest—heck, the very earth —*answered* you." Pepper's face looked chalky and blotchy, her wide eyes shining in the darkness. "The ground just *spit up crystals*—"

"So? It spits up crystals *all* the time, Pepper," I

told her calmly. She stared at me, her face turning a little green. "That's precisely how mining works."

"Not *all at once!*"

"Okay, so this was faster," I shrugged.

"It's more than that!" she yelled. "No one did that. No witch or person. No one decided and *did*. There was *nothing* out there. You literally asked nature for something and the world *rearranged itself* to give it to you. That's...that's...I don't know *what* that is, but that's..."

I realized as I listened to her it was the first time that Pepper had seen something she couldn't interpret. Not at all. She had done such a vast amount of study into the occult, had such a broad reservoir of knowledge from books that she presumed she could categorize and quantify anything she happened across, especially if she did it with me in tow.

"Can I ask you something personal?"

Pepper looked at me and nodded.

"Are you religious?"

"Am I...*what?*"

"Okay, spiritual. Do you believe in God? A higher power? Gaea? Anything like that?"

"I don't know," Pepper answered after a lengthy pause. "I don't believe in the God Dexter Kane preaches about, *that's* for sure. Fire and brimstone and judgment and hypocrisy."

"There's more to metaphysical beliefs than what Dexter Kane preaches." I rolled my eyes. "Look, I've lived in a place actually *in between* realities. Seen creatures that have *long* been considered nothing more than myth. Spoken to them. I've seen gods with my own two eyes. Even after all that, there are things I can't explain, that magic *doesn't* have the answers to."

"What are you saying?" Pepper asked, tilting her head.

"Just that every time you ask a question and get an answer, you'll find another question behind it. Another mystery. You saw something few people ever get to see," I told her. "Enjoy it. Don't ask too many questions. Just value the experience."

"Fortuna, have you *met* me?"

FIVE

I could see the light in the parking area off in the distance when Pepper tripped and went tumbling onto the ground for the third time that night.

"Damn it," she cursed. A car door banged noisily. Within moments, a powerful engine roar echoed all the way into the woodland.

"What the heck did I—oh, no." Pepper scurried to her knees and felt for a pulse on the guy she had just tumbled over.

"Oh my gosh," I choked. "Is he okay?"

"He's not breathing, but...look, he's warm to the touch. Maybe he just had a heart attack." Pepper flung down the book and started performing CPR on the man. I started to help, but she waved me off.

"I've got it," Pepper told me.

I feared Pepper's efforts would be futile. Looking around the clearing, I spotted an enormous quartz crystal covered in blood near the man's head and there was a pool of something on the ground beneath him.

"Pepper, look." I pointed with one hand and grabbed her lightly with the other. "I don't think he had a heart attack. Maybe the earthquake came all the way out here. He must have tripped and landed on the rock."

She shifted and looked, then pulled her hands away from the lifeless man so fast I could scarcely see the movement. "Step back," she ordered me and brought herself to her feet.

"Okay." I backed up, then hesitated and peered at her. "Why am I stepping back?"

"Evidence," Pepper told me. "Don't get any of your fibers, DNA, or *anything* else on him."

"Pepper, you're being ridiculous—"

"Am I being *electrocuting-angel-statue* ridiculous?" she challenged me, her right eyebrow lifted. "How about *twenty-year-old corpse-in-your-wall* ridiculous?"

"You don't think—"

"Let's make sure, Fortuna, that's all I'm suggesting."

"I don't believe this," I told her, skeptical. I

peered at the deceased man sprawled across the clearing. "I *can't* afford to shut down while they investigate me for murder *again*."

"I'm going to call Ga—the police." Pepper drew out her phone. "Looks like we'll be out here a bit longer, so find a comfortable rock."

* * *

"What did the two of you do now?" Gabe said when he spotted us on the path. Bobby Newsom, the lackadaisical county coroner, and his associate, Ollie Kane, followed with a stretcher. Newsom looked like the effort it took to walk the quarter mile into the park from the parking lot *might* give him a heart attack.

"Nice to see you, too, Gabe," Pepper answered him, her scathing tone masking the pain I could detect in her eyes as she stared at her ex-boyfriend. "We were just out for a stroll and stumbled across him. Like, literally."

"What were you two doing hiking in the woods this time of night?"

"This is Tom Wilson," Ollie Kane said before Pepper could respond. The kindly coroner's assistant hunched over the body examining it gently. "He's the postman that delivers to the outskirts of town in the hills. We used to play pool together at Stick's."

"You know if he's got any people?" Bobby Newsom asked him.

"Yeah, his parents live just off the square. Hey, Fortuna, Pepper." Ollie smiled at us. "Was he still alive when you came up on him? See anything?"

"We didn't hear anything when we were walking up here. I tripped over him when we were leaving," Pepper said.

"Was he here when you started your *hike*?" Gabe asked, forcing a particular intensity on the word hike to get across that he *clearly* didn't trust we were on a hike.

"Yeah, Gabe, we skipped over the dead body because we didn't wish to delay our evening," Pepper retorted, incensed. "No. He wasn't here when we came in."

"Had to ask, since you two aren't known for your concern for others," Gabe mumbled. He stared down at his pad and made notes.

Pepper's jaw fell.

Bobby Newsom had been leaning with his elbow on the gurney, glancing back and forth between Pepper and Gabe. Lighting a cigarette, he took a long draw and emitted a choking cloud of smoke. "Someone want to let me in on what's the issue here?"

"No," Pepper and Gabe snapped simultaneously.

Bobby raised an eyebrow and twisted toward me. "Miss Delphi?"

"Gabe and Pepper are not getting along very well at the moment, Mr. Newsom."

"Well, *that* much I could sum up all on my own," Bobby replied, taking another long drag off his cigarette. Ollie continued to study Tom Wilson's dead body and the space surrounding him. Bobby's stained shirt was tight, and it had lost enough buttons that his furry belly peeked out over his belt. "What about you? What do *you* think?"

"What do I think about what?" I asked, mystified.

"Hear anything, see anything?" he inquired.

"No, sir," I told him politely and shook my head. "When we arrived, we didn't see anyone else in the forest. When we came out, he was just lying here, dead. There was an automobile in the parking—"

"Uh huh," he said and belched, cutting me off. The man sent his lit cigarette to the woodland floor and stomped it out. "Well, I see nothing suspicious out here, Detective," he told Gabe. "Dude tripped, smashed his head on a fancy rock, perished. End of story. You object?"

"I haven't even taken a complete page of notes, looked into—"

"Looked into what?" Bobby asked him sharply. "Rocks," he pointed. "Stumbling. Head goes whack. Guy gets dead." Bobby Newsom burped again and shrugged. "Ain't the first time it's happened out here with these crazy rock diggers. Won't be the last, either."

"Don't you think we should at least investigate, sir?" Gabe asked him through clenched teeth.

"We did. We talked to them," Bobby pointed out. "We're gonna take the body and look at it. But we're in the forest, a rock hit 'im in the head. I mean, seriously, Detective, who do you think would want to kill *a mailman*? You honestly want to put time into this?"

"I do," Gabe told the man decisively.

"Well, you can't. I'm ruling it a mishap." Bobby spun away from us and took off walking down the path toward the lot. "Help Ollie get him into the refrigerator, will you?" he called over his shoulder in that gravelly smokers' voice. "I'll deal with him tomorrow. I was watching the game, and I'd like to get back to it before someone spoils it for me. You and Ollie can go tell his parents."

The county coroner lit another cigarette as he left the park.

"That's it?" I peered down at Tom Wilson's

ashen face. "There's a rock next to a guy and his head's bashed in, so he must have done it himself by accident?"

Abruptly, a vision slammed into my mind so fast and so forcefully that I was knocked off my feet. Pepper and I both were lucky that no one raked the forest floor—considering we kept crashing into it.

I had a nebulous vision of the tree across from me, and then pain, and suddenly black. As I cast about to steady myself, it started again—the tree, pain, black. The agony was so real my hand rushed to the back of my head to make certain I wasn't bleeding. It took place once more.

Then it stopped.

I panted on my hands and knees. Pepper and Gabe rushed to either side of me, frantically yelling my name.

"Stop! I'm fine!"

"You are *not* fine, Fortuna, you're as pale as a sheet!" Pepper said. Gabe tilted my face and stared intensely into my eyes.

"Her eyes are dilated," Gabe told Pepper. They helped me up off the ground and started to put me on the gurney brought for Tom Wilson.

"Oh, heck, no, you're not!" I shook them off. "I am *not* laying on the dead body gurney! Nope. Not gonna happen."

"You talk to ghosts, but you're frightened of

dead people?" Gabe asked me. "That makes absolutely *no* sense."

Ollie Kane stared at me, his eyes large.

"I'm not *afraid* of deceased bodies," I said, shoving him away. "It's the symbolism of the thing. I'm not laying on a gurney meant for the dead. Period. The end."

"Gabe, leave her be," Pepper told him.

The detective dropped his hands resentfully and gawked at Pepper before he spun and strode away. "You don't need my help? *Fine*. What else is new?"

"Gabe! Gabe, look—"

"Ollie, what have you got?" Gabe asked his buddy, ignoring Pepper.

"A body I have to take to the morgue, dude. You heard the boss." Ollie stood up and glanced at me again before turning his eyes back to Gabe. "It was an accident. Other than cleanup, we're finished here."

Gabe argued with Ollie that they should investigate more, and Ollie calmly deflected, explaining they had their orders and Bobby Newsom outranked them.

While they argued, Pepper leaned into me and murmured. "What happened?"

"I don't know," I shook my head, and described to her the vision I saw.

"You think it's Tom Wilson?"

"I don't see him here," I told her, searching around. "I can't say for sure, but the pain was exactly where his head seems to be cracked. At least I *think* so."

"Let's turn him over and make sure," Pepper suggested.

"I will not! And neither will you!"

"If he was standing and looking at the tree when it happened, though—"

"He *couldn't* have tripped and fallen," I told her, nodding. "I know."

* * *

"This is a beautiful crystal." Ollie deposited the large, bloody smoky quartz into a plastic bag he got from his van and tagged it. "Since Bobby doesn't think he was murdered, I doubt it will be very useful, but I can't just leave it here. We can at least establish for sure that's what killed the guy."

"Don't you get frustrated?" I asked Ollie. Pepper and Gabe stood some distance away, speaking animatedly near her car.

"Frustrated?" He looked startled. "With what?"

"With your boss's apathetic attitude toward his job."

"I grew up in this city, Fortuna." Ollie banged

the broad doors closed on the coroner's van. "As I got older, I recognized that Daddy made a lot of excuses for the things that happen here, but he wasn't the only one. He was honest about one thing, though."

"What's that?"

"If you can't change it, no point in getting upset over it. You ever heard of the Serenity Prayer?"

"Yes," I nodded, and Ollie recited it word for word.

"That's my approach to this town," he said, then twisted to look at Pepper and Gabe, both indignant and still excited as they quarreled. "Because *that's* what results when you don't have the savvy to appreciate the difference between what you can change, and what you can't."

* * *

"I can't *believe* he said that to me," Pepper fumed as we rode back toward the town proper. "How could he say that to me?"

"What did he say?"

"Never mind."

I lurched to miss a young deer that bounced into the road, but our near miss didn't break Pepper's internal catalog of recriminations against Gabe.

"Apologize. Like *I* should *apologize*. The nerve!"

"Apologize for what?"

"Just drive, Fortuna."

Eventually, I quit asking Pepper questions. It was clear I would hear no answers.

"You know what I think?" Pepper asked.

"That you can't believe he said that to you and you shouldn't have to apologize?" I suggested while I rounded into the town center and made my way to the parking space behind my shop.

"Way to be supportive," Pepper said as we stopped.

"I'm supportive of you, Pepper. You're just not giving me much to go on, here."

Pepper glared at me and forced the door wide so hard that I was shocked it didn't fly off and into my van.

"Do you want your keys?" I asked, holding them out toward her.

She slammed the door and strode toward the building angrily.

"I suppose not," I replied to no one. I joined up with her at my delivery door. She frantically tossed things from her handbag and onto the blacktop.

"What are you doing?"

"Looking for my keys!"

"Pepper, *I* drove your car!" I informed her

loudly, holding her key chain out to her. "I tried to give them back to you, and—"

"Damn it!" she screamed. She yanked the keys from my hand and jabbed them violently toward the lock. "How does he manage to make me *so unbelievably angry*! We saw this thing tonight that was amazing, we got this secret book, and all I can think about is *how much I want to beat Gabe over the head with it!*"

I cringed as the key scratched the door.

That was not going to buff out.

SIX

"Pepper seemed a few cans short of a six-pack last night," Spike told me the next morning while I nibbled at my breakfast alone. "What was she going on and on about? It was such gibberish I just disappeared and flew to the park to get some peace."

"We turned up a body in the woodlands, and Gabe was the one that showed up to investigate. Well, I say *investigate*," I declared, using air quotes, "but the whole business seemed like anything but an investigation."

"You found a *body* in the *woods*?"

"Yeah, but honestly, Pepper's meltdown last night after we got back didn't have much to do with the body," I conceded, spooning cereal into my mouth. "I don't understand why, with a gazillion detectives, we *always* seem to pull Gabe. I also don't know what happened between her and Gabe last night, but whatever he said to her set her off."

"What *doesn't* set her off?" Spike asked and rolled his eyes.

"How come you can't see recently deceased people?" I asked Spike. "All the ghosts at the Magical Midway could see each other, and when someone died, it looked like they popped up pretty quickly."

"What are you asking me for? You're the witch, I'm just a ghost," he answered, eying me carefully. "Shouldn't *you* be revealing all of this to *me*?"

"Well, maybe I'll be ready to after I dig into that strange book." I pointed toward the leather-bound volume recovered from the crystal altar last night. I explained to Spike how Pepper and I had gotten it.

"That's the *freakiest* thing I've ever heard."

"I got it. Honestly, if I hadn't been there, I'm not sure I would've bought the story."

"Why aren't you studying it?"

"I can't open it." I laid down my spoon and stepped over to the book. Reaching out, I struggled to draw the cover up. The tome was sealed shut as if it had been shrink-wrapped. "It was open when we got it, but once we shut it? It's stayed sealed."

"Can't you work a magic spell or something to make it open?"

"If I can, I don't know what it is," I confessed. I went back to finish my cereal. "If Pepper can't figure something out from one of her books, I'll go talk to Miss Bessie about it. Which is fine, you know —I need to talk to her about what's going on with Gabe and Pepper, too, though. I've backed off hoping it would pass, but it seems like it's just getting worse."

Just then, the front door buzzed.

"I wonder who that could be?" I asked Spike, and he shrugged.

* * *

"I thought you might like it." Ollie Kane passed me the smoky quartz.

"You thought I would like to have the crystal that *killed* Tom Wilson last night?" I asked him, incredulous that he had come up with this idea before it was even lunchtime the day after the thing killed a man. "*Why* would you assume that?"

"I don't honestly know, man," Ollie said, grinning. "They were just going to throw it out, and something told me you would like it. It was like this nagging idea in my brain that I couldn't get rid of, so I brought it over here."

I peeked down at the smoky quartz. Tom Wilson's blood had been washed off of it, and if you didn't realize what it had done, you wouldn't have discovered a hint of it. It was a magnificent crystal, at least a foot tall, maybe four inches wide. It had clusters along the base.

"Well, thanks, I guess?" I told him.

"So, I kinda had another agenda in coming here," Ollie replied, shuffling his weight from foot to foot as if he was somewhat uncomfortable. "That whole thing last night with Gabe and Pepper. I've watched them argue before, but last night was *epic*."

"She stayed here until late last night because she was too agitated to go home," I admitted. "I don't want to act like Gabe doesn't have a reason to be upset with us. If it was my grandma, and something he did got her in a room with a gunman, I'd probably be pretty upset, too. But he's been friends with Pepper since they were children."

"He's *loved* Pepper since they were children. Whatever the two of them tell you about being over each other? Yeah, don't trust it." Ollie leaned on the counter. "If Mystic's End became a soap opera they'd be the unfortunate couple in the center of the drama that everybody roots for—even though nothing ever works out for them."

"So, what *was* your agenda in coming over here?" I signaled for Ollie to sit. "Was it just to inform me that Pepper and Gabe are having troubles? Because I could tell that on my own."

"I figured you could," he smiled sympathetically. "I don't really get involved in Gabe's life all that much. I mean, he's my best friend and I care about him, but I try not to intrude, you know?" Ollie frowned. "Part of being a best friend, though, is recognizing when it's time to interfere because things have gone too far. After watching them last night..."

"You feel like it's time to interfere?"

"I do. Gabe is miserable," Ollie admitted. "He's missing one of the most significant folk in his life. His Gram's about to smack him upside the head for how he's acting. Miss Bessie also notices, by the way, that *you're* avoiding her again. She figures it's out of respect for Gabe."

"Miss Bessie's pretty shrewd."

"Yeah, well, she's not overjoyed about it."

"I'm new here, Ollie, and I don't appreciate all the ins and outs of people's relationships yet. But what I *do* know is that I don't want to come in between a family, you know?"

"Your disappearance is coming in between them more than your presence ever could," the long-haired coroner's deputy informed me earnestly. "That's kinda why I dropped by. I appreciate that you're avoiding Miss Bessie out of deference to Gabe, and I get that and all. I absolutely do."

"But?"

"But stop it." Ollie grinned. "I'm *not* new. I've been around these families since I was knee high to a beetle. You can't back off and give them time to quiet down and expect them to. They can pump their own heads full of steam just fine all on their own."

"Do you think there's anything I can do personally to help Gabe get over—"

"Himself?" Ollie laughed. "Just stop allowing him space to simmer in his own juices, Fortuna. Everybody's standing by for Gabe to get over himself. I expect everybody's offered him more than ample time, more than enough respect. It's time for Gabe to grasp that he's driving everybody else crazy. That's *my* two cents, anyhow."

"You think that'll change anything? What if it just makes it worse?"

"I don't think he'd be carrying on the way he is if he understood all the grief he was causing, but right now, he can't see it. He can't see it because everybody's protecting him from it," Ollie nodded. "Time for that to stop."

"Okay then," I smiled and thanked him for the suggestion. "You have excellent timing, I have something I need to meet with Miss Bessie about, anyway."

* * *

I was opening up the shop after Ollie's departure when Liz raced in. "What's wrong with Spike?" she demanded, her tone apprehensive.

"Nothing, as far as I know. Why?"

"I keep getting 'help' on the ghost message app," she informed me, holding up her phone. There were two specks on the circle at the top. Below, in the square where the ghost words are indicated, it said *Help me, Help me, Help me*.

Looking around, I noticed nothing out of place. What's more, Gideon was snoring loudly in the corner. If there was something awry with the ghost, I had no doubt the dog would rush around in a frenzy. Gideon had become incredibly attached to Spike. "He was upstairs the last time I saw him," I told her. "Let's go find out."

We started up the stairs as Spike was turning around the corner to descend. "Are you okay?" I quizzed him.

"Well, I'm dead, so *technically* I presume the answer is no," Spike told me as we approached the landing. "But since I've been a ghost for twenty years now, I expect the answer is yes. For a dead guy, I'm having a decent day. Why?"

Once I revealed to Liz what Spike had said, she responded.

"Because of the words you left me on the app." Liz held up her phone and waved the screen in the air away from herself. Spike moved back and forth, trying to read. Finally, I reached out and held Liz's wrist stable so Spike could see what she was talking about.

He frowned. "I didn't send you those messages, Liz."

I repeated what he said word for word.

"Of course you did, who else would send me messages on a ghost app?"

"Another ghost?" he suggested, shrugging.

Turning to Spike, I raised my eyebrow. "What do you mean, *another* ghost?"

"I can't be the *only* disembodied soul in this town, right?"

"You're the only ghost I've seen."

"You're assuming you can see everybody all the time. You couldn't see Hugh Maddox when he left his body, could you?"

"Well, no, but I don't know *when* that was," I told him somewhat more defensively than I wished to. I was still kind of touchy about my lack of witch prowess, truth be known. And Pepper's *half-a-witch* crack last night had done nothing for my self-esteem. "He could have left his body after I took off from the party. Or so fast I didn't see it."

"Or you may not be capable of seeing every ghost that exists everywhere," Spike answered. "There's a double dot on that app, Fortuna. As far as *I* know, I'm the only ghost here."

"You don't really think that thing can check for *actual* ghosts, do you?" I asked Spike.

"It can pick up what I say, so..." He held up his hands. "Look, I've been dead for twenty years. That phone looks to me like more mind-blowing magic than *you've* got, if you want to know the truth. The whole concept seems nuts to me. It's got no cords."

"Thanks."

"Any time."

"Help me," the app droned.

"Well, that *wasn't* Spike," I told Liz. "I'm staring right at him and he said nothing. When did it start?"

"Just a half an hour ago."

"Help me," the app droned again.

"Okay, so, let's work to figure this out," I told the two as we went downstairs. "Maybe that app can pick up the position of ghosts. Maybe it can't. But I don't see anything and I don't even know where to look."

"What do you want to do?" Liz asked me.

"Let's have Spike drift through the shop. We can take each level one at a time. Whenever it looks like Spike and the other dot are in the same area, we can start checking that area to see what's going on."

"It can't tell us what level it's on?" Spike asked.

"It's a free app that shows the location of ghosts and spells out what they're speaking with a phone. How much do you really expect it will do?" Spike looked offended. "Look, I'm sorry, let's just get this done, okay?"

"Fine. How slow do you want me to walk?"

"Liz and I will follow along behind you and we'll tell you to slow down when it looks like you're near the indicator for the other...whatever."

"Got it."

Spike wandered through the storefront as Liz and I accompanied him and observed the phone screen. An elderly man walked by the windows and looked in, frowning at us.

I imagine it *did* look a little weird.

"That's really close," Liz said. "You are practically *right* on top of it."

Spike looked around and shrugged. "I don't see anything."

"Oh no," I whispered. Spike was standing in front of the counter. Directly behind him was the smoky quartz crystal that Ollie had brought me.

"What?" Spike asked.

"Oh no. No no no no no," I whispered again.

"What is it?" Liz asked.

"It can't be. There's just *no way*."

"Would you *tell us* what you're muttering about?" Spike asked me with exasperation.

I walked through Spike and stared at the crystal. "This is the crystal that Tom Wilson hit his head on. Or got hit in the head by. Or dropped it on his head. I don't know. But this rock killed Tom Wilson last night."

"It's me," the app said.

"Tom, can you hear us?" I asked the rock.

"Here. Trapped."

"Are you *literally* stuck inside the rock?"

"Yes."

"Whoa," Liz whispered. She stared at the quartz. "Are you telling me the guy's soul is trapped in that rock?"

"Help me," the app said once more.

"Wow," Spike said, staring. "And I thought being trapped in this *building* was bad."

SEVEN

"Getting your fortune told, Liz?" Pepper asked as she strolled in the store. Liz and I went on staring, mystified, at the smoky quartz crystal between us.

"There's a dude in there," Liz told her.

"What do you mean 'there's a dude in there'? I thought you were a lesbian?"

Liz turned and glared at Pepper. "I am, and I'm *not* having my fortune told. I mean Tom Wilson's soul appears to be caught in that rock."

"The ghost app picked up somebody asking for help," I clarified for Pepper. She dropped her bags and ran over to peer deeply into the center of the massive crystal. "The app claims that Tom Wilson is trapped."

"Help. Me."

"Are you positive that Spike's not playing a joke on you?" Pepper asked us suspiciously, swiveling her head to get a better view.

"While I concede this sounds like the type of thing he would do just for funsies, I don't think so." Liz stood up. "Fortuna says she can see him and he's not doing it."

"Why would I puppet some dead guy's voice?" Spike asked. Gideon sat patiently at his feet. "I play jokes that are amusing. This doesn't seem very funny."

"How would someone get trapped in a crystal?" I mused out loud. I picked up the rock and turned it over in my hand.

"Stop. Dizzy."

"Oh, sorry," I murmured. I put Tom Wilson's temporary celestial home back down on the stand. "I've never heard of anything like this."

"Well, I haven't heard of anything like this *explicitly*." Pepper gestured toward me. "But there's a bunch of legends around crystals. The Inuit believe that Labradorite was formed when the northern lights got trapped in ice—so, like, there're some hints you can *trap* things in them, I guess."

"That's just a primitive myth, though, right?" Liz asked.

Pepper shrugged. "I read another book once,

too, that said smoky quartz is one of the best stones to work with when you're trying to work with ghosts that are caught on this plane. He seems *pretty* caught."

"I don't think that's what that meant," I pointed out.

"Can you see him?" I shook my head no. "Can you use some of your witch magic to try to, I don't know, jerk him out somehow?"

Liz pulled back and gawked at Pepper. I froze.

For someone that used every waking moment to dig up other people's secrets, Pepper *sure* had trouble keeping them.

"What?" Pepper glanced up at Liz as if she did not understand why our purple-streaked friend was suddenly peering at her like she had sprouted another head. I noticed the tough reporter didn't so much as cast her eyes toward me. Not for a second.

"What did you mean, her *witch magic?*" Liz asked Pepper.

"You live next to her and you don't know she's a witch? Sometimes I think I'm the only one in this city that pays attention to anybody."

"Pepper, you honestly don't know when to keep your mouth shut, do you?" I snapped, my face turning crimson hot. "Look, I don't like to reveal my religious beliefs," I told Liz quickly attempting to cover. "It's a conservative town, you know—"

"Just tell her," Pepper shrugged again. "What does it matter?"

"Would you *shut up?*"

"Look, Liz, she can see ghosts. Obviously, that's not the *only* thing she can do. I mean, that would be ludicrous, wouldn't it? Her name is Fortuna Delphi, for goodness' sake."

"Pepper!" I clenched my hands so I wouldn't strangle her.

"Look, I'm getting *really* tired of hiding stuff from friends, and if you *weren't* my partner, frankly, I would've blogged about all the things I've discovered you can do long ago." Pepper said with a matter-of-fact tone and a haughty toss of her head. "After last night, after the earth opened up because you *asked a question?*" Pepper crossed her arms. "People have a right to know who you are and what risk you present, don't they?"

I fumed silently as Pepper outed me to Liz, uncertain of what to do. The ghost captured in the crystal seemed like an inconsequential issue compared to Pepper's sellout of my confidence.

"What?" Pepper raised her chin.

I was hyper-mindful that Pepper Stanford was going through a terrible time—between what she saw in the wood last night, the way Gabe was treating her, and having tumbled over a dead body

—but that *didn't* give her the right to reveal my private business.

Not that she looked to appreciate that.

Liz glanced back and forth between us extending her palms, her face wary. "Look, Fortuna, it changes nothing—"

"No. You're incorrect. Her being *dishonest* changes things, right?" Pepper said with a toss of her head as her eyes boiled with outrage. "You live next to her, you see her practically every day, and you have no idea who she is. That's wrong. Right?"

Liz looked bewildered. "If I cared what her spirituality was, Pepper, I would have asked—"

"It's not her spirituality, Liz," Pepper spat fiercely. "She's not even *human*. You're friends with someone that's not even human."

Liz and I gawked at her.

"What is going *on* with her?" Spike asked.

"Look, forget it, evidently the only one who cares about any of this stuff is me," she announced, spinning on her heel and racing out the door.

* * *

Lucky for me, Liz had dismissed Pepper's sudden venomous disclosure of my paranormal identity as just one more Pepper Stanford tinfoil-hat conspiracy theory.

With a hasty hug and a guarantee I would keep her apprised of the plight of the spectral letter carrier in the smoky quartz, she went back to her salon to perm someone's hair.

"I will have to go see Miss Bessie now," I told Spike as I delicately deposited the smoky quartz crystal into a carrying carton, closed the top, and carefully raised it. "I *could* have used Pepper's encyclopedic occult knowledge to figure out what's going on. Unfortunately, she's lost her freaking mind."

"Didn't you say her and Gabe had an argument last night?" Spike sailed to the front window and peeked out onto the street.

"Yeah, she was rambling when we got back. I mean, *you* overheard her." Spike nodded. "It never got much clearer than that. It was even less precise when we were driving here from the forest. If you can believe that."

"Putting Pepper aside, what are you going to do about Mr. Postman?"

"Like I said, first I will go over to the home and talk to Miss Bessie. I need to learn if this is some weird Mystic's End thing where people die and get captured in crystals. Maybe she knows."

"If it was, I'd know. I mean, *I* didn't wind up in one."

"Maybe you have to be near them?" I

speculated. I leaned against the table. "That could be why you've never seen another dead person hanging around. There's a bunch of crystals in this town. Maybe they're all storing people."

"You don't really think all the dead people are trapped in crystals all over the place, do you?" Spike asked, shaken.

"Seen stranger things," I shrugged. "I don't know. I wish I could tell you more, but I have no idea."

"Being stuck in this building doesn't seem so bad anymore," the ghost shuddered and glared at the package like it was stuffed with seething snakes. "I wonder what it feels like to be caught in a crystal?"

"You can ask him when I get him out."

* * *

"There's my puppy," Miss Bessie cooed as a wiggling, wagging Gideon rubbed against the old woman's lap. "Who's a good puppy? Who's a good little greyhound? What a good dog," she informed the ecstatic hound, rubbing his ears.

"I have a question," I said as I laid the carton down gingerly in her private suite.

"Finally! That only took you five months!"

"No, I don't mean—"

"What do you want to know first? Why you were left behind? What the deal is with this town? Where you got your telepathy? What the mystic is?" Miss Bessie rapid-fired suggested questions at me. "C'mon, hit me, Fortuna."

"Do you know Tom Wilson? I think he's a mailman."

Miss Bessie blinked. She eyed me up and down and angled her head. "A mailman? You want to know about a *mailman?*"

"Yes," I nodded. "Actually, you know, it doesn't matter if you know him or not." I picked up the smoky quartz out of the pack and set it on the narrow table between us. "He passed last night, out in the woods. And I think he's stuck in this crystal."

"I feel you're leaving out a sizable part of the story here." Miss Bessie contemplated the smoky quartz warily. "Why don't you start over from the beginning and tell me what took place, and why you think that?"

With a deep sigh, I told her the entire situation from beginning to end. I left almost nothing out— not the earth opening up to present a leather-bound volume to me, or the unfortunate clash between Gabe and Pepper.

Miss Bessie's expression transformed when I recounted the book's appearance—but *just* as fast, it flattened out again and communicated nothing. She didn't ask me questions about it, and once I got past that part of the drama she didn't return to it.

"Pepper outed you in the midst of the discussion? Just like that?" Miss Bessie asked after I conveyed this morning's festivities. I nodded, and she exhaled. "That poor young woman. She could start a fight in an empty house, I tell you what."

"I wasn't pleased."

"Well, of course you weren't," Miss Bessie said. "That *was* the goal, I suspect. Whatever Gabe said to her last night, it made her feel bad about herself, poor thing. I've seen it before. Even though she could find a whisper in a whirlwind, that girl, she's soft underneath it all."

"Pepper *soft?*" I laughed. "Are you sure we're talking about the same person? Pepper Stanford? *That* Pepper?"

"Your friend Pepper Stanford is one of the smartest people in this town. The problem is this town is not the type of place that appreciates people like her. Gabe *always* did, though," Miss Bessie nodded as she rhythmically petted Gideon's head in her lap.

"Until he didn't. I mean, they fought all the time. Or so they both tell me."

"Well, of course they did," she nodded. "But he always *respected* her. He may not like what she does or the way she does it, but Gabe always respected her. I think this time," the old woman sighed, "he's just gone too far. He's pushed so much that now she doubts herself. When she doubts herself? That girl is the *queen* of laser-focused self-inflicted wounds."

Gideon barked.

"Doesn't happen too often, thank goodness," Miss Bessie told Gideon. Then she looked up at me. "But if I had to guess, I'd say it's happening now."

"Wait a minute—you think she did that on purpose to deliberately cause a rift between us?"

"She's never had a best friend before, not a close girlfriend like you. I think my Gabriel said something to her last night," Miss Bessie nodded to herself, gazing out the window. "He said something that got her *all* riled up and turned around in her head. And it made her want to push you away."

I sighed. "So what do I do?"

"Find out what it is. Oh, it's possible she'll regret what she did and come back—she can be self-aware when she *wants* to be. But if not, you'll have to find out what happened last night between her and Gabe."

"I can't ask Gabe. I'm not exactly his favorite person these days, either."

"Yes, dear, but he doesn't *love* you—and if you remind me I said that the next time I tell you to marry Gabe, I will deny *ever* saying it," Miss Bessie said, the corners of her eyes crinkling. She exhaled loudly and then lowered her voice to almost a whisper. "You should talk to him. Maybe *you* can get through to him, because *I* sure haven't been able to."

We sat quietly for a few minutes. Gideon soaked up the old woman's attention. Suddenly, she wiped her eyes and sat up straight, pointing to the smoky quartz crystal.

"So, I'm sure you've surmised that Tom is stuck in the crystal," she explained, repeating what I told her as if she discovered it herself. "Someone clearly bashed him in the head to kill him, and you have to help him get out."

"Well, I kinda realized that—"

"Did you *want* my help or not?" Miss Bessie asked caustically.

"Yes, ma'am," I nodded. "The question I have is how I get him—"

"Solve his murder, *obviously*."

It didn't seem so obvious to me.

"Bobby Newsom ruled the death accidental," I told her. "The county doesn't even think he was murdered, so how am I supposed to do that? I can't tell them about the visions I saw of him standing when he was hit. And Gabe wasn't allowed to do any investigating, so there's not much to go on."

And Pepper and I were in a fight, so she couldn't steal—um, borrow—the case file.

"Fortuna," Miss Bessie clicked her tongue. "Hugh Maddox's death was ruled accidental, too, and you and Pepper didn't have *any* problem figuring *that* one out."

"Yeah, but I knew those people and I had a reason to be around them. I don't know Tom Wilson."

"Well, he's right there," she pointed. "You have your app. Talk to him. Ask him questions. Go figure it out."

EIGHT

I had just made it to the lobby of Mystic Memories Senior Living when Rick Taylor, the handsome nurse that helped me set up the art show, stepped in front of me. His face was harsh, and his eyes looked troubled.

"Hey, Rick, how are you?" I asked while I balanced Tom Wilson's package—um, the box that held the rock that held Tom Wilson—in one hand and Gideon's tether in the other. When he didn't respond, I continued, "Thanks again for all the help with the art show the other night. I genuinely appreciated it."

"Right, right, no problem at all," he answered. He frowned more profoundly and leaned in. "I wonder if you'd mind stepping over there in the alcove with me for just a second? I have a question that I'd prefer none of the residents overhear."

"Sure."

Rick pressed his lips together as we advanced toward a narrow, out-of-the-way space off the central lobby. Leaning his lanky frame down toward me, he asked me softly, "Is it true that you and Pepper found Tom Wilson's body last night?"

"It is." My hip vibrated. Before I left Miss Bessie's room, I had turned on the *Ghosts, Ghosts Everywhere* app so Tom could communicate with me, and muted the voice. Judging by the near-constant notice of a message being reported, Tom had a lot to say at the moment. "Was he a friend of yours?"

"He was really active in the rock hound group I go out with a lot when I want some company. He and his wife," Rick nodded and suddenly hesitated. "Well, ex-wife. I think."

"You think?"

"I know he and Emily were splitting up, but I'm not sure if the divorce was final or not."

Interesting. Divorce seemed to be an excellent possible motivator for whacking someone on the head with a rock.

"They looked like they were still friendly, though," Rick continued, dashing my hopes that I could determine what happened to Tom in a single discussion. "I'm going to stop by and see her after work and make sure she's okay. Do you know what happened to him?"

"I don't, really." The phone's vibrating became even more frequent. "Could you excuse me for one second? Someone's sending texts over and over, and I want to make sure there's not an emergency."

I placed the carton down gently on the windowsill and pulled out my phone. Tapping to pull up the app, I thumbed through the words.

"Go. See. Emily. See. Emily. Tell. Emily. Stuck. Go. See. Her. You. Go. See. Her. Please. Please. Bring. Me. Emily."

With no context of emotions, no intonations, no sentiment, there was no suggestion at all whether this was a furious demand or a heartbroken plea. Whatever *else* this app was, it was frustratingly flat —providing just enough information to get some inkling of the ghost's communication, but not enough to understand it.

"Sorry about that," I told Rick and blanked the screen.

"No problem. Hey, I just had a thought," Rick said, shifting his weight. "I know this may sound weird. Any possibility you can go over there with me?"

"Me? You want *me* to go with you?" I asked, surprised.

"Yeah, well, I don't want the visit to seem like I'm hitting on a widow the day after her husband died if they're still married," Rick pointed out. "You know how this town is with gossip. And to be honest," he said, his voice lowering, "I've flirted with her before a few times. Nothing serious, but... anyway, can you?"

"Don't you have a sister or something?"

"Yeah, um, I do," he nodded, his eyes breaking off his gaze. "She, uh...she can't do it." I was about to ask why, but Rick met my gaze again. "And you *know* how the police are here. They *never* know which way is up. My bet is Emily might have some questions about what happened to Tom. Questions *you* might be able to answer."

"You don't think it was an accident?"

Rick stepped back as if he wanted to back away from the question and pursed his lips again. Looking around, he noticed a few residents angling to get closer to us, close enough to overhear the conversation.

"Look, I'm *sure* it was an accident." His eyes angled toward the gossipy old folks gathering. "Just thought it might be good for you to meet Emily in case she has questions, that's all. If you don't want to, that's fine."

Nothing about what Rick said rang of truth. At all.

And that made me powerfully curious.

"No, no, I'd be happy to help," I smiled. "What time do you get off?"

"Four. Can I pick you up?"

"Sounds good," I nodded. I picked up the box and headed toward the front doors. "I'll see you then."

"Thanks, Fortuna," Rick said. The phone finally stopped vibrating.

* * *

I dropped by the Mystic Diner on the way back to snag a bite to eat—a girl can't live on canned soup alone. Since I had Gideon with me, I took a seat out on the deck—only to find myself one table over from Ollie Kane, also eating alone.

"On your lunch break?" I sat down and wrapped Gideon's leash around the chair. Ollie looked up and smiled widely at me, nodding.

"Not much going on back at the station," Ollie replied, holding up his pickle. "The funeral home picked up Tom Wilson this morning, so nothing much more to do. How about you?"

Oh, just running around with a dead guy in a smoky quartz crystal. He's locked in my car. "Just heading back from calling on Miss Bessie and thought I'd grab a cheeseburger."

"Care for some company?" he asked, gesturing to the empty chair at my table.

"Please," I smiled.

Ollie Kane pushed himself up and clutched his plates, waving away the waitress who dashed over to help. "I've got it, thanks," Ollie told her. He balanced his salad plate on top of a sandwich and carefully stepped over. Once he settled his stuff at my table, he strode back over to his own and placed a few dollars down.

"Impressive balancing skills," I told him when he sat down.

"I used to be a waiter a few years back." He burrowed back into a Greek salad. Swallowing, he grinned, "Two plates and a glass aren't much of a challenge."

Another waitress came and set my cheeseburger in front of me. I was a little embarrassed by Ollie's healthy greens as I plucked off the vegetables and slathered the meat with ketchup.

"You mind?" he pointed to the large tomato I removed. As soon as I shook my head no, he snatched it and laid it atop his salad. "I have to admit it surprised me to see you here by yourself.

Aren't you and Pepper joined at the hip these days?"

"She tore into me this morning after you left," I admitted. I shoved the fries around on my plate. Gideon sat next to me, his body trembling with elation as he checked out my cheeseburger and let out tiny whines. Sighing, I tossed the hound a fry. "I don't know what took place between her and Gabe last night, but evidently, she's going to punish *me* for it."

"Well, *I* know," Ollie said, his mouth half full of tomato. "You want me to tell you?"

"Please," I said.

"Gabriel told her it was her fault Martin won't talk to you anymore," Ollie said, leaning back in his chair.

A thousand questions ran through my mind, but I asked only one. "And how did Gabe know why Martin decided not to talk to me anymore?"

"From what I've picked up, Martin spoke to him about it himself," Ollie lifted his shoulder in a half shrug. "They're not *precisely* buddies, but they're working on something together right now. I don't know what. I guess you came up."

I frowned. That was...weird. "So glad to hear it. Why would Gabe saying that turn Pepper into a rabid bulldog?"

"A rabid bulldog?" Ollie lifted his eyebrow and half-grinned.

I shook my head. "Okay, maybe a spoiled puppy. It wasn't quite as bad as all that, but she was pretty combative. And she did something...well, it *wasn't* like her."

"You haven't known her very long." He shoved long stray hairs that had escaped his ponytail away from his face. "Pepper can lash out at people pretty severely when she's feeling low. I think when Gabe blamed her for Martin, the implication was everything that happened—Miss Bessie, you, Martin—was all her fault. I don't know whether he said it that way, or she took it that way."

"Okay, if this is all true, why would she lash out at *me*?"

"Pushing you away to protect you?" Ollie said and then took a bite of his sandwich. "The nearest safe person to spar with? I spoke to him, not her, so I don't know. Sometimes, people just do things, you know?"

"You knew this was all about to go terribly, didn't you?" I asked him. "That's why you came to see me this morning."

"I always like to give people a heads' up if they're standing at ground zero, that's the first thing." Ollie met my eyes and held up one finger.

"Two," Ollie held up his second finger, "I knew that things had thawed enough for them to argue last night. I mean, before yesterday, Gabe wouldn't even talk to her. If they *were* communicating, I figured they would likely blow."

I nodded.

"Three," he said, shifting his head and holding up the third finger, "Gabe told Pepper that after what happened with Joe Arturo and the being held at gunpoint thing, he—Martin—realized you and Pepper would push even if it put your lives at risk. And he felt if you two pushed around *him*, to get his story," Ollie said, his voice dropping, "you had a better-than-average chance of putting yourselves in jeopardy."

"*Gabe* told you all this?" I asked him. Why would Martin think that? And even if he did, why would he suggest it to Gabe of all people?

"Well, not in so many words." The corner of Ollie's mouth lifted as if he was smirking at a joke only he heard. "Gabe's not real good at keeping secrets from me, so I get a lot of things in half-sentences."

"Okay, so...you think Pepper's abusing me because of guilt?" I proposed in a tone that showed I wasn't entirely buying Ollie's explanation—even though it fit pretty neatly in with Miss Bessie's. I did, though, sense there was more to it, a little more that no one else seemed able to see.

"Yeah, I do. I mean, *maybe* it's something else," he conceded. "I'm not psychic. Maybe it's not that at all. Maybe it's something different." He looked up and snickered. "I'm sure you'll figure it out sooner than you think."

"I doubt that," I told him as Gideon nosed into my lap, his muzzle twitching toward my burger. "No one other than you is talking to me."

"Oh, you may be wrong about that." Ollie pointed toward the parking lot.

* * *

Pepper Stanford marched up to the table, snagged an unoccupied chair from the people next to us (without asking), and shoved it across from me. Sitting down with some force, her eyes found mine.

"I'm sorry," Pepper told me sullenly. She reached across and grabbed my cheeseburger. Without asking, she took a bite. "I shouldn't have told Liz," she added with her mouth full.

"Told Liz what?" Ollie asked, his eyes sparkling with mischief.

"Oh no," Pepper replied, shaking her head. "I'm not doing this *twice* in one day," she announced, still chewing. "Fortuna would drown me."

"Well, if she did, I doubt she'd get arrested for it." Ollie leaned back and moved his plate out of Ms. Grabby Hands' reach. "Half the town's wanted to see you in a ditch at one time or another, Pepper."

"Ollie!" I choked, appalled.

"He's *right*, you know," Pepper told me, nodding, utterly unbothered by the idea that hordes of townspeople would love to see her dead.

"Still, that's an *awful* thing to say."

"Pepper and I have known each other for years, Fortuna," he said, looking at me. "She knows I'm just joking."

"Yeah, you're such a *funny* guy," Pepper remarked with an eye roll. "Why are the two of you eating together, anyhow?"

"We were commiserating on how difficult it is to be best friends with you and Gabriel, respectively." Ollie stretched his arms above his head and sighed. "I have to admit it's kind of nice to have someone who sympathizes with what I'm going through for a change."

"I sympathize!" Pepper told him. "I was Gabe's partner for *years*. I sympathize fully with what a judgmental, haughty, hubristic, highhanded, cocksure, overbearing—"

"Did you consult a thesaurus when coming up with that catalog of attacks?" I asked her.

"—pompous, smug, self-centered, puffed-up, vainglorious—"

"I think she did," Ollie said.

"—jerk he is!" Pepper finished. She reached over and grabbed a fry from my plate.

NINE

Once Ollie left to go back to work, Pepper was much more restrained than she had been. We remained in silence for a while, her eyes flitting from the table to my face and back again.

"So," I said, leaning forward. Pepper's fingers tapped restlessly on the table.

"Yeah, so," she mumbled and darted her eyes to look at me briefly.

"I accept your apology—"

"Thanks—"

"*But*," I said, cutting her off before she could sweep what she had done off the table, down to the floor, and decisively under the nearest outdoor rug. "Just because I can forgive you doesn't mean I can ignore it, and all is just fine and dandy. I need to hear *why* you told Liz about me. That was one heck of a betrayal, Pepper. I hoped I could count on you."

"You need to learn to curse," Pepper observed.

"You need to acknowledge the question," I told her with a level gaze she couldn't entirely meet. "I need to know whether I can trust you or whether I can't."

"You can! I mean...okay, I suppose you can't right *now*. And I get that, but...I don't know, it just came out," she sighed, tears filling her eyes as she peered at her tapping fingers. "Look, one fact you need to recognize about me. I *hate* secrets."

"That doesn't give you the right to unmask all of them," I pointed out.

"Maybe it should!"

"That's one of the most megalomaniacal things I've *ever* heard you say," I differed sharply. "It's not up to you to tell other people who *I* am, Pepper! Do I honestly have to tell you that? That's my choice and my right. I'm not some article you're working on."

"Secrets hurt people," she insisted indignantly. "Did you know that secrets can lead to stress, anxiety, depression, alienation, low self-esteem? So, you know," she added, meeting my eyes, "if you look at it in a *particular* light, what I did was actually about making sure that you didn't feel bad about yourself!"

"I feel fine about myself," I responded. "How do *you* feel about *yourself* right now?"

"We're not talking about me."

"We *are* talking about you. Stop trying to turn this discussion back on me. If you wanted to examine my choice to not tell some people all of who I am, that should have been a conversation between us. Not an outing of—"

"Liz didn't believe me, anyway. I saw her when I was—"

"Not the point. You're making excuses," I told her. "I'm not asking about the *repercussions* of what you did or if there was any harm. I'm asking you, flat out, *why* you did it."

She leaned back and exhaled, her face distressed. It was as if she was unsure of why she did it or was uncertain whether to tell me the reason. After a few minutes sitting in the mid-day sunlight, she glanced up and shrugged.

"You're more self-aware than that."

"Look, there wasn't just *one* reason, okay? Gabe swears up, down, left and right that Martin stopped speaking to you because he was worried about you getting hurt. I guessed maybe if he knew you were a witch, he'd realize that you can take care of yourself."

"So you told *Liz*? Uh uh," I shook my head no. "Try again."

"It's true!" You wouldn't have expected it to look at Pepper, but she had an unusually expressive face. Most journalists' faces remained stoic, detached, given the unpleasant stories they frequently have to report. A practiced distance. Not Pepper. Her concerns, her attitudes were printed large across her face and in her eyes.

"Maybe that was a modest part of it, but it wasn't the *fundamental* part," I told her calmly. "I want to know *why* you did it. Everyone has spent the morning telling me about your self-immolation tendencies when you feel lousy about yourself. Was that it?"

She squinted. "Yeah, sure, I was trying to push you away," she agreed cheerfully. "You know, to protect you. I do that sometimes." Pepper looked pleased to latch on to this second excuse.

"Or you were furious at me for leading to the estrangement between you and Gabe," I responded. "And hurting me like that, betraying me, was a way to get back at me."

Her face dropped as guilt suffused her expression. I could sense her cringe from the accuracy of what I suggested, a truth Pepper had shoved away all morning trying to persuade herself what she had done was in pursuit of principle, of reconciliation.

"Look, I don't need you to admit it. I can see that I'm right just by the look on your face," I told Pepper. "I am sorry that what I did caused us to be in the position we were and that Gabe is having such a rough time with it. You've taken the brunt of his resentment, and I *am* sorry for that."

"He's not talking to you, either," she pointed out.

"Yes, but I don't really care," I answered.

"You do."

"You do too care about Martin not talking to you."

"I care about the dead guy imprisoned in a thick quartz. And being able to depend on my best friend to hold my secrets until I'm ready to share them. Martin and Gabe? They can wait."

* * *

I knew that Pepper wasn't ready to concede that her lashing out at me was, at least in part, vindictive and spiteful, but I let the exchange at the diner drop once I could see in her face she understood what she had done. I didn't actually need an apology—I needed her to comprehend her motivations so she *wouldn't* do it again.

I had always known Pepper was impetuous, and no one's inclinations are driven by good *all* the time. I couldn't fault her for that. It was, after all, very human.

"So, that's the end of it," I said. While driving her back to my shop, I had wrapped up all I had picked up that morning. Pepper had walked to the diner, and her car was parked behind my store. "Miss Bessie thinks we have to solve Tom's murder for him to leave the smoky quartz."

"Why?"

"I didn't ask." I didn't mentioned I'd tried.

"Why not?"

I shrugged. "It doesn't really matter if Miss Bessie's right."

"Yeah, but what if she's not right?"

Gideon barked.

"Well, then we'll know after we catch his murderer—which I would guess you'd want to do regardless of whether it pries him out of his special rock."

"Right. So, I looked into Tom Wilson," Pepper said, carefully shifting the box on the floorboard so she could pull her pad from her backpack. "He is, or was, thirty-four when he died. Graduated high school, no college," she read from her notes. "Married Emily Banner fresh after graduation, no children. His friends circle consisted mostly of other postal workers, and since this is a small town, there are only five of them. They all have alibis—they were at Stick's playing pool. The bartender said they were there all night."

"What about his rock digging friends?" I asked her.

"Yeah, so, that's where it gets a *little* harder to track," she conceded, flipping through the pages. "There's a group Tom was a member of that was, like, pretty loose. No membership lists or dues, just a loosely affiliated group of folks. Then a team he was a part of—*that* was less loose."

"A team? What does that mean?" My phone was silent as I asked, and it surprised me—Wilson had been pretty chatty until the past hour.

"It's kind of like a pool, I guess? Well, not, like, a wagering pool. More like a cooperative. He had an arrangement with two other people that they'd split the profit of whatever they found and sold."

"You find any legal suits or anything between them?" I opened the car door and stepped out.

"Nope, but I got their names," she called over the roof of the car. "William Johnson and Lucy Miller. Johnson runs a rock shop on the outskirts of town, and Lucy Miller drives a tow truck for Bannister Towing. Lives next door to him. Her nickname is Lulu."

"How did you get so much information so fast?" I asked her, impressed.

"Irma Sperling," Pepper said. We carefully removed the box with Tom Wilson in it. "That old librarian is my secret weapon."

Pepper held Gideon's leash and unlocked the rear shop door for me so I could carry the box in without having to balance it on my hip. As we walked into the front room of the store, I glanced up to find Vito Salvatore staring at me through the storefront window. He smiled at me and waved from the sidewalk.

Behind him? An uncomfortable-looking Martin Salvi.

Great.

"Oh, for goodness' sake, *not* today," I groaned, set the box down and went to unlock the front door to let in Martin and his Uncle Vito.

* * *

"Need more paint," Vito's gruff, gravelly voice announced as he pressed into the shop. "More colors, more brushes, more canvas. More of *everything*, really. The best you have."

"I can help you, Mr. Salvi," Pepper called. She set her backpack down and glimpsed Martin. "I've been hanging around here long enough that I know where most everything is."

Vito stopped and suddenly half-smiled, peeking back toward his nephew, and again at me. "You think I could test out the paints in the back, there, young woman?" he challenged Pepper mischievously.

"Absolutely! Follow me, there's a mess of paint back there."

"I'll be a while," Vito told Martin, dramatically swinging his hand. "Old man like me, I do things *slowly*. Especially when I get to have the attention of a beautiful girl while doing it." Pepper blushed. "Slow, Martin. *Capisce?*"

They retreated into the back. I wanted to kill both. Lord knows if I did, it would doubtless be determined an accident and I'd get away with it, considering this town's spotty law enforcement history.

Well, depending on the day and Bobby Newsom's mood, I guess.

Martin cleared his throat. "Nice to see you."

"Is it?" I spun away and straightened up the back counter. "I wouldn't have expected so, considering your face when you saw me. But sure, I can bluff, too. Nice to see you, too, Martin."

I heard him breathe slowly, but I didn't turn around.

"Can I get you some coffee while you wait?"

"Look, Fortuna, you have every right to be—"

I whirled on him before he could complete his sentence and pointed my finger at him. "If you are about to give me the *approval* to feel my own feelings, Martin, you can just *save* it," I said coldly. "I don't need *your* permission to feel what I feel or think what I think."

Martin lifted his eyebrow and looked at me for what seemed like an eternity. I glared right back. Then he nodded but added nothing. I turned away again.

"Just sit and wait for your uncle."

"My uncle is going to keep coming back here until I apologize," Martin conceded.

"That's fine with me. I actually like your *uncle*." My voice dripped with sarcasm. "Besides, you already apologized."

"But you didn't accept it. Not really."

"I accept it. We good?"

"Nothing about this is good," Martin told me sadly. "And I realize that it's all my fault."

I laughed shortly, a single harsh laugh. "Then work through it so you don't make the same mistake again, and good luck to you on your journeys," I told Martin. "I don't know what you want me to tell you, Salvi."

"Tell me you'll have dinner with me," he said—

in a total and complete about-face so sudden I felt like I had whiplash. I turned and stared at him.

"*Dinner* with you? Are you *kidding* me?"

"You're right, I owe you an explanation. I'd like to—"

"That was my stance *last* week. This week, I don't care anymore," I lied. I cared, but not enough to revisit this while I was lugging around the postman in a quartz crystal. "The only thing I really care about is you staying out of Gabe and Pepper's relationship. Stop talking to him so that the two of them can patch things up."

"If I get him to talk to her, will you go out to dinner with me?" Martin challenged.

Could he be any more manipulative?

"I'm not *bargaining* right and wrong with you, Martin. You'll somehow lessen the rage he feels for her, because it looks like *you* fed it, and because it's the right thing to do. With the guarantee of nothing in return," I declared in a sharp voice. His eyes held mine. "If you do, then maybe—only *maybe*—I'll consider hearing your explanation."

Uncle Vito picked that very point to re-emerge from the back. The old man announced that he needed some time to think about which paint was the right paint for him and told me he'd come back. With Vito snapping at him, the greyhound track manager glanced at me once more and accompanied his uncle out.

"So, your phone's dead," Pepper told me, holding up hers. "Tom's been talking to you pretty steadily. Which is good, because we need to ask him about an eight-hundred-pound crystal cluster he found."

TEN

"So, how did *that* go?" Pepper and I settled down at the table, Tom's crystal between us. I scowled at her. "What, your and Uncle Vito's little disappearing act that caused Martin and me to talk? That 'that'? Did you guys rehearse that or just come up with it on the spur of the moment?"

"Uncle Vito's an unusual guy," Pepper shrugged. She jerked her chair forward without answering. "It sounded to me like he gave Martin a what-for and a who-for and a you-better all at once."

"You. Stop." Pepper's phone boomed.

"I think Tom's annoyed we've been neglecting him. Which we haven't," I declared loudly toward the rock. "My phone lost charge. Probably because *you* were talking non-stop."

"That's awesome," Pepper beamed.

"What is?"

"That we're a *we* again."

I looked at Pepper, who was smirking as if she was twelve and had just won the school spelling bee. "So, I don't want you to take this the wrong way," I said patiently, "but have you *ever* thought about therapy?"

"I have a psychoanalyst, thank you very much," she told me proudly.

"Do you *go*?"

"Are. You. To. Done," Pepper's phone interjected.

"Oh, don't get your trousers in a twist, Wilson." My impetuous friend thumped the crystal. "You're dead. You have all eternity to work out your issues. *I* don't."

"Show some compassion, will you? And just a reminder, there isn't a statute of limitations on murder."

"Yeah, well," Pepper tossed her hair. "It's not like it's *our* responsibility to help him, you know. We're doing him a favor. He could be a *little* more grateful. Though to tell you the truth, I'm doing this for the byline."

"Grateful. Now. Help."

"Well, you're welcome," she smiled.

"Was. Not. Thanks. Help. Me."

"Demanding for a dude locked in a rock, don't you think?" she huffed.

"What were you talking about before?"

"Which time?" Pepper asked me.

"The crystal cluster?"

"Oh, right," Pepper leaned down, tugged out a thin newspaper and shoved it toward me. Skimming, I recognized it was the local tourist newspaper that the Chamber of Commerce put out highlighting fun attractions and shops to visit in Mystic's End. "That's Tom," she pointed to a grainy image on the paper's front page. The dead man, smiling broadly, stood next to a *mammoth* table-sized crystal cluster.

"Wow, that's huge."

"And valuable," she nodded. "I stopped by the rock shop after I got that from Irma. Bill Johnson, one of the three partners with Tom, said that mega-crystal is worth about a quarter of a million dollars. It's on exhibit at his shop."

"Is this one of the shared-ownership rocks that the team splits?"

"So, that's what I want to talk to Tom about, if I can," Pepper said, leaning toward the phone. "Bill claimed that the three of them—Tom, Bill, and Lulu

—disagreed about whether it was one of the split ownership rocks."

"My. Crystal," the phone interjected.

"Yeah, he mentioned you'd say that," Pepper nodded. "Well, he doesn't realize you can still talk, but he pointed out that you felt the crystal was dug up *outside* of the zones that all three of you worked on collectively."

"A quarter of a million dollars split three ways? That's eighty-three thousand dollars each," I said, calculating quickly in my head. "People have *probably* bashed other people in the head with a rock for less."

"No. Money," the phone droned.

"What do you mean, Tom?"

"I think what he means is whether Tom agreed or disagreed, it was a moot point," Pepper told me. "Bill said that Tom was adamant that he *didn't* want to sell it. Not at any price—and their arrangement only kicked in when they *sold* something. It was a once in a lifetime find, and he preferred to hang on to it and leave it to his children."

"What children? I thought he didn't have any children."

"Emily," the phone said, but it included nothing else.

"I thought Emily and Tom were breaking up?"

"About that. They're legally separated," Pepper explained. "Not divorced."

"Emily," the phone said again.

"Well, we're in luck," I told Pepper after the phone said nothing other than Tom's wife's name. "Rick Taylor, the attendant from the old folks' home? He asked me to go with him this afternoon to call on Emily Wilson."

Pepper frowned. "Why?"

"They all went out together and dug up rocks."

"No, I get that. I mean, why you?"

"He thinks Emily might have questions about what transpired when Tom was found, and since I was there, he assumes I can answer them," I shrugged. "That, and he's flirted with her before. He also thinks bringing me might ward off any scandal that he's hitting on a widow the day after her husband died."

"No. Rick," the phone's monotone voice rang out.

"Why not?" I asked the crystal.

Silence.

"Is he not talking, or is the phone just not picking up his messages all the time?" Pepper asked me.

"How would I know? I still don't see how it's doing what it's doing." I picked up the phone and peered at the solid green speck in the chart. "It didn't pick up everything Spike said—maybe every third word or so. And frequently, when he talked, it would snag only one or two words out of full sentences. I have no sense of how much we're getting."

"Okay, so let's presume that Tom Wilson *won't* be all that much help." Pepper pressed her palms together and looked up. "You go with Rick this afternoon to interview Emily and see what you can find out. I'll go to Tom's apartment and poke around and see what I can find out. We'll meet back here for dinner."

"I think Tom lived alone," I told her.

"So?"

"So, if he lived alone, how...You know what, never mind," I told Pepper as I got up. There wasn't a trespassing law created or bolted door made that could keep that woman out.

"Emily," the phone said again.

"You going to bring the rock?"

"I probably should, but honestly, I don't know how to explain to people why I'm lugging around the crystal that killed Tom Wilson. That seems strange even for this town."

"I doubt anyone realizes what that smoky quartz is," Pepper pointed out. "Everyone knows you were a fortune teller, Delphi. I don't think seeing you lug around a crystal is as peculiar as you think."

* * *

R ick Taylor stepped into my shop just as two visitors were taking off with their new purchase, one of Azalea's oil landscapes. His eyes were deep-set, and the sense of sadness coming off him seemed genuine.

"I really want to thank you for agreeing to come with me," Rick said.

Gideon pouted. I brought the greyhound almost everywhere with me these days, but I didn't think bringing him to the home of someone I didn't know was a good idea.

The dog openly disagreed.

"No problem, Rick. Gideon, I'll be back in two hours, and then I'll give you some bacon to make up for it, okay?"

The greyhound's melancholy face and droopy ears perked up.

Rick and I walked out the front door toward a black, muddy Jeep, and he politely held open the canvas door so I could climb in the lifted off-road vehicle.

"Sorry about that." Rick helped me settle in. "I need the clearance when I go out on the trails to the more remote digging sites. It's not the most comfortable daily driver in the world, but until I strike it rich, I can only afford one car."

"Not a problem," I told him. "I've been in less comfortable vehicles."

Really, to be honest, once we drove I couldn't think of a *less* comfortable vehicle. The truck's ride was so loud and so violent I had trouble determining whether the rattling I was hearing came from the motor or my teeth.

"You should let me take you off-roading," he yelled over the wind and engine roar. "I bet you haven't been that far outside of town. The mountains are magnificent."

"I've been on the walking trails—"

"Oh, right, when you found Tom," he cut me off. "What were you and Pepper doing out there so late at night, anyway?"

I didn't recall telling Rick what time we had gone hiking, and I turned to look at the handsome nurse.

"We just went for a walk, that's all," I hollered back.

"Were you going anywhere in particular?" We rounded into an older suburban development.

"Just to see the trees."

His eyes darted to the side at me and then back to the road.

"Are you cagey on purpose, or do you just not enjoy answering questions?" Rick called out.

"I'm not cagey. I don't enjoy shouting," I screeched.

"Fair enough," he roared back.

Once we slowed down enough that we could have had a conversation, Rick did not take up his questioning.

There was something about what he asked me that put me on alert. I didn't know Rick Taylor well, but he seemed like a nice enough guy when we interacted once a week at Wrinkle City. We pulled up in front of a charming suburban home and I wondered how he learned where Emily Wilson lived.

"Does she know we're coming?" I asked, climbing down out of the tall SUV.

"I didn't call her, no." He came around and glanced at the large bag hanging off my shoulder. "What's that?"

"My bag?" I suggested as if the answer was obvious.

"That thing is huge."

"Art supplies," I added as we turned to trudge up the driveway.

I had cleared out art supplies from a knapsack with a flat bottom so I could haul around Tom Wilson without anybody realizing he was in there.

Well, okay, no one but me, Liz, and Pepper knew he was in there. But it was a good size crystal, and I couldn't think of a suitable reason to explain why I was carrying it around with me.

"She's home," he announced as we stepped onto the stoop and buzzed the doorbell.

* * *

"Rick!" a short, pixie-like woman with blotchy red skin opened the door, an expression of bewilderment on her face. Her eyes were swollen as if she had been crying all day, crushed up tissues stuffed in her hands. "What are you doing here?" she asked.

"I heard this morning about what happened to Tom," Rick said, his tone falling to a gentle, soothing baritone. "I wanted to come by and tell you how sorry I was, and to see if you needed anything."

"Who are you?" Emily's blue eyes locked on me. "Do I know you?"

"No, ma'am, I'm just an acquaintance of Rick's."

"This is Fortuna Delphi, Emily." Rick angled toward me and planted a hand on my shoulder. I frowned and took a small step to the right. His hand slipped. "Fortuna found Tom last night in the woodlands. I assumed you might want to meet her."

Emily's eyes grew so enormous that I thought her eyeballs would pop out of her head.

"*You're* the psychic!" Emily gasped and her hands fluttered to her midsection. "You're the psychic that moved into town a few months ago!"

"I've done psychic readings in the past, yes, but I own an art studio now," I responded, but halfway through my sentence, the tearful woman reached out and yanked me into her house by the arm. Rick followed.

"Tell me if he suffered," Emily pleaded with me, her voice choked by sobs. "Psychics can talk to the dead, right? Have you talked to him? Is he still around? Do you know if—"

"Emily, please, sit down," I told the shaking, sobbing woman. I brought her to the sofa. "Let me get you some water." I strode toward the kitchen, hoping to find a minute to think.

I was in a predicament.

Most people don't believe in psychic or paranormal phenomena, not really—but Emily *clearly* did. On the one hand, I could tell her I was in contact with her husband and that he was all right. Maybe it would bring her some comfort.

If she *needed* comfort, I reminded myself. It could all be an act to throw off suspicion.

On the other hand, her husband *really* wasn't all right. He was confined in smoky quartz after being smashed on the head, and I didn't know who did it.

This woman just inherited a quarter of a million-dollar crystal cluster. Despite her evident emotional turmoil over his death? She was still a pretty good suspect.

You can discover whether it's an act in two seconds, I heard Pepper say in my mind as clearly as if she were standing there chastising me for my uptight psychic integrity. My impetuous friend would have dug around in Emily's head like it was a grapefruit, and she had a magic spoon.

This *wasn't* life or death, though.

I had made an oath to follow the principles that Priestess Goodfellow taught me. What good is a vow if you just *break* it?

I walked back toward the sofa with a cup of water and resolved to figure out what was going on in the old-fashioned way—as my phone repeatedly vibrated on my hip.

Okay, *mostly* old-fashioned.

ELEVEN

"Thank you." Emily smiled at me, the grief echoing through her expression. "I'm sorry, I didn't mean to...I've just been so... Anyway, I'm sorry for confronting you like that."

"Are you alone?" I asked, peering around at the empty, silent home. Shelves displayed pictures of Emily and Tom in kayaks, with friends around a felt-covered table at the casino complex, seated with an older couple at a kitchen table that wouldn't have looked out of place in the nineteen-fifties. Interspersed between the numerous framed prints were crystals I presumed Tom had discovered.

"My parents are on their way from Oregon," she explained. "They should be here later on today."

"Do you have anyone that can stay with you until they get here? Tom's parents, maybe?" Emily winced at the mention of her in-laws. "I'm sorry, are you no longer on good terms with Tom's parents?"

"Is it really proper to question her like this, Fortuna?" Rick asked sharply from across the room. His pulse beat in his neck as he looked at me with his arms crossed. "She just lost her *husband*, for goodness' sake."

Well, *that* was an overreaction. Rick's sudden aggression was unsettling. I had said nothing out of bounds to Emily. What was I missing here?

"I was just worried that there's no one here with her, Rick, that's all. It's never a good idea to go through grief on your own if you don't have to," I said, shifting away from him and back to her. "I just thought that you and the Wilsons could help one another through this devastating time."

"Oh, I don't think the Wilsons would want *me* around." Emily put down the glass, tears still shining in her eyes. I could see her hands tremble ever so slightly. "Mama Wilson was especially upset when we split up. She suspected that *I* had cheated on *Tom*."

"Did you?" I asked without thinking.

"No, no, I would never do that," she responded, her eyes casting over toward Rick and again back to me. "Tom had such a wonderful relationship with his parents, though, I don't think he could bring himself to tell her the truth about why he left."

"If you don't mind my asking, what *was* the truth?" Rick stared at me again, but he said nothing.

"I guess there's no point in hiding it now. Tom was the one that was unfaithful, not me," Emily half-smiled. She struggled to play off the announcement as if it didn't upset her, but I could see her muscles tense. "We were taking some time apart so he could work through...well, whatever midlife crisis he was going through. I don't think we would have divorced. At least, I *hope* we wouldn't have." She took a deep breath and exhaled harshly. "I guess now we'll never know."

The phone on my hip vibrated again and again and again.

"I'm sure things look bleak right now, Emily, but you have to remember that Tom loved you," Rick told her while I dragged out my cell and checked out the ghost messages. "And you're absolutely not alone. *I'm* here," he said to her with a compassionate smile.

Emily nodded and returned the smile, then swung back to me almost instantly. "You found Tom in the forest?"

"Pepper Stanford and I found him, yes," I told her. She closed her eyes and grimaced again as if imagining the incident in her mind.

"I know I was a little...anyway, you're a psychic," Emily spoke then, leaning toward me. "Did he suffer? Do you know? I've been playing what the police told me over and over in my mind, and all I can see is—"

Rick jumped to embrace her as a sob choked off Emily's words. She leaned against him for a moment, just a moment, and then forced him away.

"Emily—" Rick started, but the slight woman held her hand up.

"Please," she fixed me with her stare. "Please, if you *really* are psychic, if you really know, please! Please tell me."

I stared back at her. Then I inhaled.

I *could* tell her.

I could let her know there was a flash of pain and surprise, and then darkness. In the grand scheme of things, it *wasn't* an excruciating death. Tom Wilson barely had time to process what was happening to him before he was gone.

But if I told her, *it* would start.

The looks on the street from those that were suspicious of people with a sixth sense. The constant visits from individuals who demanded to know lottery numbers, or whether their partner was cheating, or whether their girlfriend loved them.

It was almost always the same questions, and I *didn't* want to deal with them anymore.

But these questions...

Questions like the one Emily was asking me were important. Was it fair I hid who I was, what I could do? Was her peace of mind and comfort *less* important than my keeping what I could do a secret?

It was, after all, for *my* comfort I did it.

Looking into her anguished eyes, the storm of dread and fear discernible, I suddenly felt selfish.

"He didn't suffer." I shook my head. "He had only a momentary perception of his injury before he lost awareness. There was barely enough time for him to understand what was happening to him, or to feel any pain. I assure you, he *didn't* suffer longer than the second it took him to register the blow. Then he was gone."

"Really?" Her voice was hopeful. She folded her palms around her midsection and exhaled. "Are you sure?"

"I am," I responded.

"I'm so glad to hear you say that," Emily said, breathing with relief. "It doesn't make it better, but it makes it...easier to take knowing that he didn't lay on the forest floor suffering after he tripped."

"Tripped, right," I muttered, staring down. When I glanced up a few seconds later, Emily was staring at me with suspicion.

"He tripped...right?" she asked.

"I...um..." Shifting uneasily, I reached down to grab my phone again. "I think I have a text, one second."

"Fortuna?" Emily pleaded. "Do you know something about how Tom died?"

Sure, it starts with an *assure me he didn't suffer*. It inevitably goes into *who killed him*, or *where is the life insurance policy*. Next?

Lottery numbers.

"Sorry, I honestly have to get this text.".

"You know something," Emily said. She leaned forward and clung to my wrist as I was bringing my phone up from my bag. "What do you know, Fortuna? Did you see something with your psychic thingamajig? Something different from what the police said happened?"

"I didn't see what happened to him with my psychic thingamajig." I gently wrested my wrist from her grip. "I saw maybe a second or two through his eyes, that's all. And...it's just that...well, he was staring at a tree. Straight on, up and down. Not sideways."

"What are you saying, Fortuna?" Rick asked me, heat staining his cheeks. "The police said that Tom tripped and fell and hit his head on a rock."

"I know that's what the police said," I acknowledged. "I'm saying that from what *I* saw, it looked like Tom was standing up when he was hit from behind."

* * *

"*Why* did you tell her that?" Gabe asked me. We stood outside of Emily Wilson's house.

Emily was so astounded by what I'd said that she called the police to let them know she had new information. When Gabe showed up and heard what that new information was...

Well, let's just say he was *not* amused.

"What are you even *doing* here? Do you have any idea what you've just done?"

"Told the truth?" I returned. "Look, she *asked* me, Gabe. I didn't want to lie to her."

"You didn't have to *lie* to her, you could have just *not* told her, Fortuna. You were there last night. Bobby closed the case, it's an accident, *end* of story. He's going to be furious if the widow runs around screaming about a murder because *some art teacher* got a vision from the great beyond."

"Pepper runs around screaming about a murder all the time and it doesn't seem to faze him at all, so I *doubt* that."

Gabe's indignation seemed to coil around him. "I will not talk about Pepper with you."

I glared at him, fed up with whatever drama he had convinced himself was going on in his head.

It was enough.

I tried to understand Gabe's concern and give him time to get over it. I attempted to exercise as much sympathy for his position as feasible.

For *months*.

I was done.

Standing in front of that house? My empathy ran out.

"You know, Gabe, you guys can ask everybody in the town to lie about what they know or what they think just so we can live in the reality the Mystic's End Police Department wants to *pretend* we live in, all right? But the fact is *none* of us have to," I told him, bitterness filling my mouth. "If you stopped and looked at everything that's happened since I arrived here? It hasn't been *my* fault. It's been *yours*."

"*My* fault?" he asked, his face contorting with annoyance and astonishment. "How can you blame me for—"

"Yes, brainiac, *your* fault," I sputtered. "Your department doesn't do its job, and you are *part* of that department. Miss Bessie never would have been in that room if you people had just *investigated* Hugh Maddox's murder with an open mind. But you *didn't*. I probably wouldn't be here, by the way, if Bobby Newsom hadn't sauntered out of the woods declaring that *nothing* had happened when I knew for a *fact* that was a lie."

"I don't run the department, Fortuna!"

"You're just following orders?" I suggested sarcastically.

"And you don't know *anything* for a fact!" he said, raising his voice. "All of this is just in your head! It could be your imagination."

"Oh, yeah?" I pulled out my phone and shoved it in his face. "I know things for a fact. *This* isn't in my head."

Gabe pulled his head back and his eyes focused on the screen. Scanning over the words, his eyes widened. "What is this? What are you showing me?"

"The words of Tom Wilson, newly departed."

"What are you talking about?" he asked, his voice softening.

"This app can pick up the words of ghosts," I explained to him. "Not all of them, and it's not the most dependable thing I've ever seen, but enough of 'em. Tom Wilson is stuck in the smoky quartz rock that killed him."

"And you know this how?"

"Because Ollie brought me the rock," I told him, dropping my phone. "And it's a darn good thing that he did, considering the fact that this poor mailman is locked up in it because someone murdered him. So, *as usual*, Pepper and I are trying to do *your* job so we can help him get to where he needs to go."

Gabe's face twisted in confusion.

"If you're going to help, then *help*. If you're going to continue to live in this fake bubble the MEPD keeps this town wrapped in, then get out of my way," I fumed. "Because I have to tell you, Gabriel? I've just about had it with *all* of you."

* * *

There was an almost fearful silence between Rick and Emily when Gabe and I stepped back in the house.

"You're not going to investigate anything, are you," Rick said. It was more a statement of the obvious than an actual question.

"Tom's death has been ruled accidental," Gabe told the two. "Technically, no one from the police department should look into it anymore. Barring any new evidence, the case is closed."

"But Fortuna has new evidence!" Emily pointed at me. "Tom was standing up when he was hit!"

"That's a psychic flash from a carnival fortune teller," Gabe said matter-of-factly, in a *far* more insulting way than was needed. "I don't say that to be disrespectful—"

Sure he didn't.

"—but because that's what we will consider it. That's not *evidence*. The police department does not formally recognize psychics as a source of information."

"And why would they?" Rick said, glancing at me. "As I was just telling Emily, the probability that what popped into *her* mind has *any* meaning at all? That's ludicrous."

I presumed that Rick was no longer interested in dating me.

"Rick doesn't believe in psychics," Emily said, her tone apologetic. "*I* do, though."

"The necessary part of this is that the Mystic's End Police Department does not," Gabe interjected, heading off a debate about whether psychic phenomena were real.

"Well, I'm *not* a member of the police department," I told Emily, electing to drop any pretense about why I was there. "And I want to know what happened. First, I have to ask you— where were you between the hours of 7 and 11 p.m. on the night Tom died?"

"I was at...I was in Little Rock at the doctor," she told me, her hands moving anew to her midriff.

I gasped out loud. I couldn't believe I missed it before.

"You're pregnant," I said. Her eyes filled with tears, and she nodded as Rick stepped away from her. "I'm not trying to be impolite, but is it Tom's?"

"Yes," she confided, nodding again. She went over to the counter and seized a sheet of paper, passing it to me. "A month and a half ago we started talking. One night...well, one thing led to another, and we weren't careful, and..." Emily began sobbing softly again. "He was so *happy* about the baby."

"He knew?" Gabe asked.

"I told him the day before he died. I had picked up a pregnancy test, and I needed to let him know as soon as possible. The night he died was my first OB appointment."

I looked through the paper. It was a doctor's receipt, dated the same day as Tom passed. The timestamp and address of the office supported Emily's story.

"Why didn't he go with you?" Rick asked, a little more judgmentally than the moment called for.

"He told me he had to take care of some things, you know, take some time to...what did he say? Unwind his interim life, he said," she wiped the tears from her face. "He told me that when he came back, he wanted to be all in. For me *and* the baby."

The three of us looked at the mother-to-be, widowed and weeping. My heart broke for her.

"I promise, Emily, I will help you with *whatever* I can." Rick went over and slipped his arm around her. "You're not alone in this."

TWELVE

"It *could* have been Bill over the enormous crystal," I chattered at Gabe in the truck as he drove me back to the store. "Or it could have been Emily over the enormous crystal since *she* inherits Tom's portion...well, or the whole thing, right?"

"*What* gigantic crystal? And what has that phone told you?" Gabe asked.

"Or Lulu, for that matter," I continued out loud, ignoring his question while I worked through the possible suspects. Grabbing my cell, I turned up the sound on the app so we could hear any observations Tom might make. "*Both* of them could be suspects. Then there's Rick, though I wouldn't have thought he could do it until I watched him with Emily. He's got it *bad* for the mailman's wife. Maybe he bashed Tom in the head with a rock."

"Just *slow down*, Sherlock, and back up a minute, will you?" Gabe said, pulling into the town plaza.

"Look, I'll let you know what I figure out. Just drop me off in front," I answered, my hand on the door handle as Gabe slowed down in front of my shop. "And thanks for the ride, even though you're not talking to me."

Gabe glared at me. "I'm *driving* you."

"That would be the first time in several months, you know."

"Look, I haven't been *avoiding* you. I just... haven't been coming around the way I did before—"

"You started avoiding me?" I joked.

"I wasn't avoiding you," he repeated with another glare.

"No?"

"No. I was avoiding Pepper."

"When you opened this little isolationist bender, Detective, you were in the throes of shrieking at me in my own home." I settled back in the seat and studied Gabe, letting my hand drop from the door. "Sure, Pepper was there, too, but you *clearly* intended some blasts to land on *my* head."

Gabe turned to look out the front window, his hand still clutching the steering wheel. I waited for him to react to what I said, but he expressed nothing.

"Look, I get that you and Pepper have a lengthy, serpentine, emotional story. I even get why you would blame me for your grandmother getting mixed up in the Hugh Maddox thing. You didn't just withdraw, though," I told him. "You sidled up to Martin—"

"That had *nothing* at all to do with you and Pepper!"

"You and Martin just stopped talking to us *on the same day*?" I asked him, unconvinced. "You both froze us out and pretended we didn't exist in the same twenty-four-hour period? It was just a fluke? How stupid do you think I am, Gabe?"

"I don't think you're stupid. The one thing I could say about both you and Pepper? You're *not* stupid."

"Apparently, we are, because she and I both felt you and Martin could handle having relationships with women who aren't wilting flowers," I told him sarcastically. "I mean, clearly, that was a *foolish* presumption on our parts."

"Shut. Up. Idiots," the app announced.

"What was that?" Gabe asked, his eyes large.

"Tom Wilson." I held up the phone and positioned the screen toward Gabe. "I imagine he thinks this isn't the time for this discussion, considering he's trapped in a quartz."

"Emily," the app answered.

"I don't think Emily clocked you in the head with a rock, *even* if you factor in the pregnancy hormones," I said toward Tom Wilson's temporary home. "What was the part of your life you had to wind down, though? The thing you had to take care of before you could get back with Emily?"

"Lulu," the app answered.

"Lulu Miller? What about Lulu?" Gabe asked.

"She was the third person in the little rock-hound trio they had," I told Gabe.

"What's in Little Rock?" he asked, baffled.

"Not Little Rock the *city*, they had a group together. All three were rock hounds. They would split the profits of the crystals they dredged up when they sold them."

"I'm not familiar—"

"Of course you're not, you people didn't examine anything. That's why *I'm* telling you," I said with an eye roll.

"You know, you're sounding more and more like Pepper." Gabe shut off the car and opened the door to get out.

"Thank you," I told him.

"That *wasn't* a compliment."

* * *

Pepper turned and brandished her stenographer's notebook at me with triumphant excitement. Her mouth opened, but just as she was about to speak she saw Gabe walk in after me.

"What are you doing here?" she deadpanned, her arm slowly slumping to her side.

"Emily called me about some new information she alleged to have on Tom Wilson's death, so I headed over to her house to find out what it was. It wound up just being Fortuna and her psychic hotline to the dead."

"That doesn't answer what you're doing here," she charged back.

"Am I not allowed to be here for some reason?" Gabe volleyed right back at her.

"I understood we were on your *Do Not Call* list."

"Well, you two are, as usual, in the middle of a controversy about a death, right? So what am I supposed to do?"

"Not investigate. You know, the same way you *usually* do. Or don't. Anyway, you know what I mean," Pepper said, her tone positively dripping with bitterness. "Just go about your merry way, remaining in your fake-news pink bubble of false happiness, Wilcox. We got this. As *usual*."

Pepper's eyes flared with ferocity as she stared at her erstwhile boyfriend across my cheerily decorated seating space in the store's front. Every word she said had been marinated in suffering before she slung it at Gabe like so many arrows.

"I realize that this is tough for you to comprehend, but I'm a cop, Pepper—"

"Of *course* it's hard for me to comprehend, Detective. I doubt you could detect the cause of crime with two hands, a scanner and an electronic beacon nailed to the suspect's—"

"You know, I'm really a decent detective! It's not my fault that—"

"Oh, don't you dare start rattling off what's *not* your fault." Pepper strode up deliberately to him, her fists balled at her sides and her eyes tightened.

"Pepper—"

"Don't you dare pretend that all of this swirls around you and you have absolutely nothing to do with it. You are a *part of the system*. Every time you follow a lead you know couldn't conceivably be right because someone told you to—"

"Pepper—"

"Every time you grab and hold on to a clue that would get the *wrong* person in trouble because someone advises you to, no matter what logic—"

"That's not how it—"

"Every time you don't challenge the truthfulness of the information being *given* to you, information that sends you off to fetch, like Clutterbuck's your master and you're a dog—"

"Now you *wait* just a minute." Gabe walked up just inches from Pepper.

"You both need to stop," I suggested after I unpacked Tom Wilson and turned.

"Fortuna, stay out of this," Pepper warned me.

"You're in *my* shop, in front of *my* storefront window, and the two of you look like you're about to come to blows," I replied coolly. "Take it down a notch and step *away* from each other, will you?"

The sound of glass breaking interrupted whatever phase the encounter was about to escalate toward. A black object sailed across the room and landed with a deafening crash.

Gideon launched himself at me and slammed me to the ground. Out of the corner of my eye, I could see Gabe had tackled Pepper and was sheltering her body with his own. His arms were wrapped around her, and their faces were inches apart. For a moment, they peered into each other's eyes.

"*Stay down!*" Gabe whispered. He drew his handgun from his hip and twisted over onto his back, his body still pressed against Pepper, muzzle pointed toward the door.

The sound of tires screeching and chains rattling echoed through the brand new break in my window. I scanned the shattered glass, trying to spot what object had destroyed it.

Four feet to my right, a massive black rock lay motionless on the floor. I pushed up and pulled Gideon on my lap away from the glass, then checked frantically to make sure the dog was uninjured. He glared at the rock and growled.

A moment passed, and then another.

"Everybody okay?" Gabe asked, then moved toward the front to peer out.

Pepper lay on the floor, not stirring.

"Oh my God, Pepper, are you okay?" I pleaded. I struggled up with the hound and lifted Gideon to the counter so I could rush to check on my friend.

"I'm fine," she murmured once I was practically on top of her. "I didn't get hit or cut or anything."

"Then why are you still on the floor?" I asked.

It was then I noticed her eyes were filled with tears, and her face burned. Reaching out my hand to help her up, my eyes filled with empathy. "It will be okay," I told her.

"I'm said I'm okay," she sputtered. She pushed up to her feet, flashed at Gabe, then back to me. "It doesn't matter, I'm okay." Pepper took a deep

breath, exhaled noisily, and stood up ramrod
straight. Scanning around, she pointed. "Look over
there, there's paper on the rock."

Without worrying about fingerprints or
evidence contamination—because, let's face it, no
one from the police department would investigate
anything—I picked up the rock and removed the
rubber band that held the paper in place.

WITCH

"Well, that's clear enough, I suppose." I showed
Pepper. Her eyes grew large.

* * *

Gabriel had gone full throttle into detective
mode. He talked to people outside to discover
if they'd noticed anything while Pepper and I
managed to clean up the broken glass off the floor.
Gideon perched on the counter overseeing the
work.

"What *happened* in here?" Spike asked, drifting
in from the back.

"Where have you been?" I asked.

"Over at Liz's," he pointed next door.

"Someone threw a black crystal through the
front window," I said, disposing of the last batch of
glass into the garbage. I turned away from the front
and murmured the spell Gunther had taught me to

clean up soot and hoped it got any residual unseen fragments left on the floor.

"What's Martin doing here?" Spike asked.

"Martin's not here. Gabe was here a minute ago and he'll probably be—" I replied as I turned, but the sight of Martin standing two feet inside of my shop, his face concerned, choked off my reply to Spike. "What are *you* doing here?"

"Gabe called me," Martin said. Jeeves, his driver/bodyguard, scanned the room. The chauffeur's brow was deeply furrowed in concentration.

"Gabe *called* you?" Pepper and I glanced at each other and she shrugged once before I stared back at Martin. "Why on earth would Gabe call *you?*"

"Check the back, Jeeves," Martin ordered his manservant. The silent man nodded sharply once and then strode resolutely toward the rear of my shop. *Without* asking me if it was okay.

"Did I enter a time warp or something?" I asked Martin as he walked toward me.

"Are you all right?"

"I'm fine, but *what* are you doing here?"

"I told you, Gabriel called me and explained to me what went on. I was in the area and I decided to—"

"Don't start this conversation off with a lie." I

pointed my finger toward his heart. "You and I both know you were *not* just in the neighborhood. Don't insult my intellect by pretending that you were."

Martin's eyes locked on mine, unshakable. I held his gaze and stood by for a rebuttal that didn't come.

"Anyone. Remember. Me," the app called from the floor.

"Oh, shut *up*, Tom," I told the pithy rock.

"What was that?" Martin looked around the shop trying to find where the mechanical voice came from. I didn't answer him.

"You need to go."

"That's not going to happen."

"It's like going around in circles with you," I replied with irritation. "You *don't* get to be the one in control here. You realize that, right?"

"I'm obviously not the one in control here, Fortuna, or we would've already talked this through. That doesn't change the fact that somebody just attacked your store, and I'm not leaving."

"We don't get to talk just because *you* decide we get to talk, Martin."

"Are you saying that you're not speaking to me because it was my idea, and not yours, to talk now? Weren't you the one asking me for an explanation just a few days ago when I was in here with my uncle? Doesn't that really make it *your* idea to talk?"

"It's not about whose idea it was!"

"What is it about then?" He inclined his head toward me, waiting.

Martin was making *my* head feel like it would explode.

I had never met someone so ridiculously good at boxing me into a corner in a discussion, and I *didn't* appreciate it. I had never dated a lawyer, but I imagined this was what it felt like when they brought their work home.

As I wracked my brain to come up with an answer, sudden and forceful images of bacon pulsed in my mind's eye. Gideon, who looked as if he were smirking, angled his head sideways to peer at me.

"Bacon," I answered.

"Pardon me?" Martin's eyebrows jumped up with surprise.

"My head is filled with bacon right now. I promised Gideon." I released the broom, spun on my heel and went calmly toward the back of the store.

THIRTEEN

"Weird day, huh?" Pepper walked into the kitchen.

"Are they still down there?"

"Martin and Gabe?" she asked and then nodded. "Yeah, they're having some kind of male-bonding meeting with Jeeves. I wanted to go someplace where things weren't so...*virile.*"

Pepper sat down on a stool and watched Gideon chase small pieces of bacon that had crumbled off and tried to get away. Her typically alert and inquisitive face was glum, her shoulders sagging, and her back hunched over while she stared at the dog.

"That must have been hard," I noted quietly.

"You have no idea," Pepper said, shaking her head. "I can still smell his cologne on me. It's the one *I* used to buy for him. Tell me *that's* not a mindf—"

"Pepper!"

"Sorry," she mumbled.

"They should have named this town Pendulum," I told Pepper. I put the bacon back in the refrigerator and closed the door. "I swear, everything in this place seems to swing back and forth at such a rapid pace that I have trouble keeping up sometimes."

"Oh, I don't know, Mystic's End seems *pretty* spot on," Pepper retorted with a smirk. "You seem like you're at your wits' end, and you're the mystic. So, yeah," she chuckled.

"You don't find this a little ridiculous?" I asked her.

"I find it *a lot* ridiculous," she admitted. "But which part? The ghost locked in a crystal? The two men downstairs that don't want to talk to us but seem to rush in *guns-a-blazing* every time we're in the slightest bit of trouble? Or the original problem that someone was murdered, and no one in any position of authority seems to care?"

"Martin doesn't have a gun," I murmured, bending down to pick up the plate that Gideon had licked clean. The dog laid splayed across the floor looking like he had just run a marathon. His half-open eyes watched us with lazy disinterest.

"Oh, don't kid yourself," she shook her head. "I don't doubt that Martin, or Jeeves, is packing."

"So, what we do? Hide up here until they leave?"

"You think we should?"

I leaned back against the counter and stared at the ceiling.

Martin was right, as much as I *loathed* to admit it.

I had pushed him for an accounting when he was here with his uncle Vito, and he had come back to give me some kind of explanation—but I rejected it, blaming Martin for Pepper's ordeal with Gabe. Demanding, even, that he fix it.

Which was, I had to admit, not much different from Gabe blaming Pepper for *my* difficulty with Martin.

Even though I didn't know if there was any truth to it.

Though Gabe seemed to know.

I suddenly realized there was quite a lot of guessing going on about what everybody knew, what they didn't, and what their motivations were for their actions.

I was tired of it.

"I think we should all sit down and talk, since we're all here," I told her, ignoring the pang of unease that gripped my stomach. "They need to decide whether they're in or out with us."

"What are you talking about?" Pepper asked, genuinely shocked. "After everything they put us through, you want to go down there and ask them to come back to us—"

"I don't want to ask them anything." I hurried over and grabbed her elbow to drag her with me before I changed my mind. "But I realize everyone needs to lay their cards on the table. Me included."

"Hold on, hold on a minute." Pepper yanked my arm back. I turned to face her and crossed my arms. "Are you saying what I *think* you're saying?"

"That I'm going to tell Martin who I am? Yes," I nodded. "I'll also ask him who *he* is. And why the two of them are working together. And if they can't be honest? Well, at least the two of them will understand why they can no longer cross the threshold of my shop."

"I don't understand," Pepper intoned, eying me with confusion.

"A spell, Pepper. I would cast a spell that would keep them from rushing in here ever again."

"You can do that?" she asked, her eyes wide.

"Honestly? I don't know." I grabbed her arm again. "But I'm darn sure they don't know, either."

* * *

I was so stunned I didn't move at first.

"Did you actually call *more* people?" I asked Gabe when I spotted Ollie sitting on the couch, smiling.

"Hi, Fortuna," Ollie said with a broader smile.

"Hi, Ollie," I said to the long-haired biker in a much more pleasant tone than I *felt* like using. Turning to Gabe again, I frowned *again*, dropping any hint of pleasantries, and spat, "*Did* you?"

"Ollie brought over the plywood," Gabe said slowly, pointing toward my now boarded-up window. He looked at me as if I were a bomb ready to go off. "While you were feeding the dog, we boarded up your window."

I should say thank you because that *was* pretty considerate of them. I should thank them for doing it.

But I didn't.

"Pepper and I want to talk to all of you." I pointed toward the rear studio.

"Can you watch the front, Jeeves?" Martin said to his bodyguard, rising to walk toward the back. Gabe and Ollie followed him silently.

"Bring. Me."

"This is *none* of your business, Tom," I told the rock.

"Enter. Meant."

"I'm glad we're entertaining your afterlife," I told him. I followed Pepper toward the back instead of heading to pick up the rock. Jeeves glanced at me without changing expression.

"Questions?"

"No, ma'am," Jeeves responded and then turned to scan the front window, or at least the *part* of the front window you could still see out of.

"Please, everyone, sit down," I gestured as soon as I entered the studio.

"I wasn't able to find anyone who saw anything which, admittedly, is not all that surprising," Gabe reported as we made our way to seats around the large craft table.

"I don't want to talk about that."

Gabe frowned. "Then what do you want to talk about?"

"Why are the two of you here?" I asked Martin and Gabe pointedly. "You've been ignoring us for the past two months. *Not* returning phone calls, going to the other side of the room when we happened to be in the same public places. Now, suddenly, you're here. Why?"

"You and I bumped into each other at Emily's," Gabe frowned.

"We did, and you drove me back, and that was great, I appreciate it. Why did you come in?"

Before he even took a breath to answer, his eyes tracked to Pepper for just a split second.

"Because you...because I...No particular reason," Gabe answered after glancing toward Ollie and Martin.

"Have you told him?" I asked Gabe while pointing toward Martin. He shook his head no. "How about him?" I pointed to Ollie. He shook his head no again.

Ollie jerked his chair up and shifted forward. "So, thing is, like, I know, already," Ollie said with a smile.

"You know what?" Martin asked curtly.

"Well, now, I can't actually *say*, can I? Because I don't know if *you* know. I don't really know if Gabe knows either, actually," Ollie shrugged. "He's said some stuff, but not everything."

"What are you talking about, Ollie?" Gabe asked him, looking perplexed.

"What do you know?" I asked Ollie, my eyes narrowing.

"You want me to speak openly?" he asked me, an eyebrow raised.

I extended my hand and gave a short nod. Martin, Gabe and Pepper stared at Ollie with rapt attention as he eyed me. After a few seconds, he nodded to himself.

"Well, see, I went to school in Austin. Don't know if you knew that. I know Samantha Goodfellow," Ollie admitted with a shrug. "Been to Avalon Grove a couple of times, too. Maybe more than a couple. So, like, I know...things about magic and the paranormal. Not as much as you, of course. But I know a few things."

I stared at Ollie, surprised. I had never picked up on any hint of recognition in the kindly deputy coroner at all. "You know who I am?"

"A little bit," he nodded. Pepper stared at the quiet, unassuming man she'd known her whole life, with her eyebrows raised and her mouth slightly open. Martin's face remained impassive while Gabe stared at his best friend open-mouthed.

"Were you trained?" I asked him.

"A little bit," he answered with a half-grin and shrugged his shoulders again.

"That's why you brought me Tom's crystal," I guessed, leaning forward. "You knew he was in there."

"Let's just say I knew there was something off about it. Something more than it'd taken someone's life," Ollie admitted. "I take it you figured out what was off?"

"More like on, or *in*. He's stuck in it."

"Oh, man, that's a real bummer," he frowned.

"You don't look surprised," Pepper said suddenly. I turned and found her staring at Martin. "Nothing about this conversation is surprising *you* at all."

"Maybe I just have a good poker face," Martin told her. He and Pepper locked eyes.

Then she shook her head.

"Maybe you're just a great big liar," she countered. "You know something. I can tell."

"Does *everybody* at this table know that she can see ghosts?" Gabe asked, looking around the table. The table greeted the question with various half-shrugs and nods.

Including from Martin.

"Among other things," Ollie told him.

"Wait, *what* other things?" Gabe stared at Ollie with a perplexed expression. "She can do more than see ghosts?"

I picked up the piece of paper from the rock thrown through the window and placed it in the center of the table. The four of them stared at it.

A second later it crumpled itself into a ball and sent itself sailing into the trashcan.

Gabe stared at the center of the table.

"You knew?" Gabe asked Ollie, his face pale. He nodded. "You, too? *Both* of you?" Gabe asked

Pepper and Martin. I wasn't surprised when Pepper nodded yes.

Martin shocked me to the core when *he* did as well.

"Who else knows?" Gabe demanded.

"Just Miss Bessie," I told him. "At least, as far as I know. Though Emily and Rick know I can talk to ghosts, I guess. Emily believes I'm psychic, but Rick doesn't."

"My *grandmother* knows?" Gabe shoved his chair back from the table. "Are you *kidding* me?"

"We are not, but that's not really important right now," I told Gabe. Martin reached out and placed a hand on his arm. "The important thing is... this is one of *my* secrets," I said, looking around the table. "And it's a *big* one. Quid pro quo."

"Huh?" Gabe sounded shell-shocked.

"Your turn," I pointed to the two of them.

* * *

I don't know why I told them what I was, really. All I can say is the effort to hide it was becoming exhausting, the dishonesty uncomfortable. The frustration and anger and fury I had at Martin for his behavior over the past two months made me realize that it was possible, just *possible*, that people I cared about felt that way about *me*.

And I didn't want them to anymore.

"What do you want to know?" Martin asked.

"Why are you two friends all of a sudden?" I asked him. "Did you just bond together in your aggravation with Pepper and me, or is there something going on?" Martin stared back at me, his face impassive. "I gave you something on me. Out with it."

"I didn't mean to hurt you." Martin sat back and shifted uncomfortably in his seat. "I know you'll never believe this, but I really *was* doing it to protect you."

I opened my mouth to snap at him, to tell him I didn't need protection from *anyone*, but Pepper reached out and placed a light hand on my arm to silence me.

"I knew what you were. Oh, not right away," Martin half-smiled. "But when I get involved with people, I...I look into them. Sure, I knew about your fortune-telling past and all that, but I didn't have any reason to believe that was legitimate. That you really *could* do that."

"Until what?"

"Until you started talking to the ghost that lives in your house," Martin told me. "I overheard you and Miss Bessie talking a few times, put the pieces together. I wasn't eavesdropping, not really, but I tend to be—"

"Suspicious?" I asked.

"Observant," he corrected. "A private investigator uncovered the rest."

"No one knows that witches are real, not really," I pointed out. "I highly doubt a private investigator would turn *that* up."

"That's not *quite* as true as you might think it is," Martin told me. "Most don't believe in witches, not as they *really* are, that's true. My family, though, is an old family. We have...contracted with non-humans in the past."

"Wait, you're *not human?*" Gabe asked, shocked.

"Oh, for goodness sake, Gabe, be quiet," Pepper hissed.

"So you didn't want to have me in your life anymore because I wasn't human," I told Martin. A muscle in my jaw twitched.

"It's not that. It wasn't some form of intolerance. I find you fascinating, Fortuna." Martin raked his fingers through his perfectly styled hair and smiled at me. Even in his discomfort, he smoldered all sexy-like. "It wasn't about you, or who you were, not really. It was about me."

"What about you?" I asked.

"More to the point, it was about my father." Martin's eyes dropped and he looked uncertain, vulnerable, for the first time since I'd known him. "I was afraid if I could find out who you were through a private investigator, so could he. And if *he* knew of your talents, he would be...concerned."

"Concerned about what?"

"Exposure." Martin raised his eyes.

"I knew it! You *are* mobbed up!" Pepper guessed. Martin winced.

"Let him finish," Ollie told her.

"I hoped when you met my Uncle Vito you would figure it out," Martin admitted. "That's part of why I brought him here to Mystic's End, that maybe you'd understand who my family was after you met him. Why I had to distance myself."

"You couldn't just *tell* me?"

"Not until Gabe made sure there was nothing illegal happening at the track." Martin shook his head. "I didn't want to risk the business unless I knew for sure that my father wasn't running some con there. This town depends on that track; I didn't want to risk people's livelihoods."

Gabe nodded, agreeing.

"And although Dad *told* me he wasn't doing anything illegal there, promised me he wasn't... Well, I needed to know for sure. Gabe was helping me with that."

"Who is your father?" I asked him, but he didn't answer. Finally, Gabe did.

"Marty Salvatore, the head of the Dastardly Crime Family."

"The *Dreamboat Don?*" Pepper asked, shocked. "The one that's in all the gossip magazines all the time? The one that dates models?" Martin nodded. "You're his *son?*"

"Firstborn and only son," he said, his eyes glued to mine.

FOURTEEN

I tapped my finger on the smoky quartz that housed the murdered mail carrier, thinking about how impossible it was to keep secrets in this small town. Even though the city seemed full of them.

"Fortuna?" Pepper's voice called quietly from the hallway. I turned. "You okay?"

"You know, when I lived in the paranormal world? There were *so* many secrets, Pepper. So many secrets, so many people out to get everyone else. Murders that happened years ago just coming to light, hidden truths, anger."

She nodded sympathetically, her eyes steady.

"I came to this town for answers, sure—but I also came to it for some *peace*. To get *away* from secrets and drama. Just paint pictures, be happy. You know?"

"You didn't check into this town well, did you?" My friend smiled sadly. I didn't answer. "So, I know that what he hid from you was a big deal."

"It's funny, it's not *that* big of a deal to me," I shrugged. "We are not who our parents are. *I* know that better than anyone. It's not who he is."

Though the fact that he was did explain an awful lot about the way he acted.

"Then what is it? Why is your face all grumbly and frowny?"

"It's what he *did*," I sighed and sat down on the floor to cuddle Gideon. The dog hadn't left my side since I got up and walked out of the back room. "It's that he didn't trust me enough to *tell* me who he was. The fact that he hid it, the fact that he acted for me without talking to me. That *is* who he is."

Pepper slid down next to me. "At the risk of getting walloped with a truth two-by-four, *you* didn't trust him enough to tell him who *you* were."

Which was the issue I kept coming back to. I was hurt that Martin chose to just disappear without talking to me, that he hid this from me as if it was some big secret. That he knew I was a witch —and never *admitted* that he knew.

"It's a valid point, and I know it seems hypocritical of me to be angry at him when I did something similar," I told her. "I'm not happy with myself at the moment. I can't exactly feel righteous indignation here, but on the other hand, I have *no* idea what to do."

"Talk to him?" Pepper asked.

"Help. Me. Get. Out. Of. Here," the phone droned loudly in a translation of a remarkably complete sentence. "Stop. Whining."

"I'm *not* whining," I told the rock.

"You *kind of* are," Pepper half-smiled.

"Whose side are *you* on?" I glared at her, but grinned back. "Did *you* know who his father was?"

"It's a gambling establishment, you know? I always suspected there was some kind of mob involvement somewhere. I didn't think Gabe was *wrong* about that, just that he went about proving it all wrong," Pepper admitted. She lifted her shoulder in a half shrug. "I *think* I told you that I suspected, but did I ever find any proof? No. That was covered up *really* well. Three years ago? It's like Martin didn't even exist."

"He changed his name."

"He did, and if Gabe hasn't found that there's anything illegal going on at the complex, Fortuna, it *might* mean that Martin changed his last name to distance himself from his family. Or, at least," she said, as she scratched Gideon's rump, "distance himself from the way they've done business in the past."

"I. Am. Trapped. Do. This. Later."

I glared at the phone and exhaled, bowing my head. "You wrote about me when I first got here, right?"

"I did. Until you told me not to."

"Telling them who I am isn't going to change much, then, right? The people in the town aren't going to treat me any different, will they? You insinuated I was a witch before I got here."

"Not many people from this town read my blog, Fortuna."

"Great," I sighed.

"The guys in there aren't going to tell anybody," Pepper assured me. "Well, Gabe might, but not on purpose. He just has trouble keeping his mouth shut sometimes."

"Common. Issue. Here. Stop. Talking. Get. Me. Out."

"He's getting better at that," Pepper said.

"Tom's also right." I scrambled up off the floor. "Everybody in that room seems interested in helping. Well, everyone but Martin—"

"Fortuna, I'm the last person in the world to tell you not to hold a grudge. I have so many I'd have to pack them in an extra suitcase just to go on vacation." Pepper pulled herself up and leaned toward me. "But that man just revealed something he's hidden from *everyone* in this town for three years. Because of *you*. Give him a *chance* to explain. Not in front of all of us. Just the two of you."

"Maybe." I walked back and pushed away Martin's revelation. I didn't know how to feel about what just happened, and helping Tom out of the quartz was a good distraction. "For now, we need to get Tom out of that rock."

"Thank. God. Finally. Cheese."

"Cheese?" Pepper looked confused.

* * *

"A re you planning on helping us exorcise the postman from the smoky quartz?" I asked the three men gathered in a circle. They were whispering to one another. "Or do we have more deep, dark secrets to tell?"

I tried not to feel guilty for asking that question.

I *did* have one more secret. Only Pepper and Miss Bessie knew I was born in Mystic's End years ago. Only the two knew I was searching for who abandoned me on the courthouse steps and why.

But...I wasn't ready to come clean on *that* one yet.

"I'm a little more concerned about the rock thrown through your window," Gabe said crossing his arms. Martin looked slightly confused at the hard right turn the meeting had taken back into ghost-rock land, but his face smoothed out quickly.

"Myself as well," Martin agreed, as if we'd never spoken about his father.

"If everyone—*other* than my grandmother—that knows you're a witch is in this room, who could have thrown it?"

"Women have been called witches by people who don't like them for *hundreds* of years, Gabe," Pepper said with a dismissive wave of her hand. "It doesn't necessarily mean there's some paranormal conspiracy coming for Fortuna, or that someone has discovered what she is."

"That may be the *least* paranoid thing I've *ever* heard you say," Gabe told her in amazement.

Pepper extended her middle finger toward him.

"Besides, a paranormal conspiracy would use lightning bolts, not a rock with a rubber band and paper," I added. "I *think* it has something to do with Tom Wilson."

"How do you mean?" Ollie asked.

"So, here's what I've discovered so far," I said, and recounted the rest of my visit to Emily Wilson's house, and the things I observed or learned before Gabe arrived. Emily being pregnant. Tom Wilson cheating on Emily. I also shared Rick Taylor's suspicious change of behavior once we arrived at the house. "If she spoke to someone after I left and told them about the 'psychic vision' I had, that someone could have driven by and thrown the rock to scare me into shutting up."

"While Fortuna was visiting Emily, I stopped by *The Rock Shop* and spoke to Bill Johnson." Pepper rummaged through her knapsack and pulled out her notes. "He seemed legit sad that Tom was dead, and there was nothing super suspicious in his demeanor, but that mega-crystal *is* sitting in his shop."

"And possession is nine-tenths of the law," I added.

"Yeah, that's *not* a thing," Gabe told me.

"There's no placard on the crystal saying that Tom Wilson owns it," Pepper said. "Just a framed copy of the article showing that Tom was the one that *found* it. Bill seemed like a nice guy and all, but he *could* claim Tom sold it to him."

"Did. Not," the app interjected.

"But he didn't claim that to you, did he?" I asked her. "You said that he told you the story about it being in dispute. Obviously, the dispute between Bill and Tom wasn't that contentious."

"How so?"

"If you thought your business partner was going to steal your big crystal find worth a quarter of a million dollars, would you give it to them to display in their shop?" I pointed out.

"That, and he *told* you the story," Gabe said. "If he killed Tom Wilson to get his hands on the gigantic rock, he would have had his story straight when you walked in. He *never* would've told you the ownership was disputed. He would've made up some story about it being his, and used you to put that story out."

"My spider-sense tells me we need to talk to Bill," Ollie said. "If we don't want to do that again because he might get suspicious, we *could* just hack into his CCTV. See what happened the day of Tom's death."

"We?" Martin asked.

"Well, *me*," he shrugged.

"You can hack security cameras?" I asked Ollie.

"You got *your* magic," he responded with a proud smile and cracked his knuckles. "I got *mine*."

"How did I not know you could hack things, Ollie?" Pepper's eyes grew wide. She looked the short biker up and down. "Boy, this really *is* a night of secrets. You and I need to talk more." You could almost *see* the computer systems she wanted to break into lining up into a list in her head.

"I was feeling a little left out," he chuckled.

"Isn't that illegal?" Martin asked Gabe, his face troubled.

"Not...not if he gets a warrant," Gabe answered slowly and then turned to look at Ollie, his eyebrow raised in question.

"I can *play* a song by Warrant while I hack if it'd make you feel better," the biker offered.

"Aren't you *technically* a law enforcement officer?" Martin asked. "How can you do something like this?"

"I subscribe to relativism," Ollie responded. "I don't know what anything *is*. I only know how it seems to me at this moment. I read that somewhere, and it makes sense. At *this* moment, hacking into his security feed seems like the right thing to do."

"As curious as I am and as much as I would love to embrace that logic, this seems wrong," I said to no one in particular.

"Many things in this town *seem* wrong, Fortuna," Pepper said. "This one's breaking *our* way. Don't look a gift horse in the mouth."

"I'm going to take Gideon for a walk." Gabe turned on his heel and grabbed one of Gideon's leashes. Turning back to us, his face tense, he looked at his friend. "How *long* should I take the dog for a walk, Ollie?" he asked through clenched teeth.

"About an hour. That should do it."

Pepper watched Gabe take the excited greyhound out the back door. "Wow," she breathed as the door slammed. "I never thought I would see the day."

"He'll unclench his butt at some point," Ollie said. He pulled out his laptop and opened it. "You'll see. It just takes time."

"Everything always takes time, I suppose," Martin said. I looked up and I found him watching me.

* * *

"Wait a minute, you're getting on *my* Wi-Fi?" I asked as Ollie connected to my network and launched a few windows with lots of text that looked like it was written in a foreign language. "You can't do this from my network, they'll trace it to me."

"Who will?" Ollie asked without looking up.

"The police?"

He kept typing. "You think the police will trace it here?" Ollie chuckled.

"Why are you laughing? It's *not* funny," I told him.

"It is." He shifted up and squinted at the screen. "You just don't know *why* it's funny."

"Okay, smarty-pants, why is it funny?"

"You're worried about The Mystic's End Police

Department Computer Crimes Division tracing it back to you?" he asked me distractedly.

"Shouldn't I be?"

"Nice to meet you, ma'am." Ollie stood up and extended his hand. I shook it, confused. "Allow me to introduce myself. Mystic's End Police Department Computer Crimes Division."

"You're in the division?"

"I *am* the division," he winked, withdrew his hand, and sat back down. "Computer crimes aren't pervasive out here. Martin's complex has its own internal division to deal with any fraud or computer crimes that might happen there, and they deal directly with the FBI. We don't go near it."

"You guys all *really* do sound completely corrupt, you realize that?"

"See?" Pepper told me with exasperation. "Quit calling me paranoid, woman. I have *ample* support for my paranoia. Including the fact that your boyfriend's the godfather's son."

Martin winced but continued watching silently.

"This isn't corruption." Ollie raised his eyes toward me. "This is vigilante justice. We're righting a wrong. Well, hopefully," he added, leaning forward again and hitting a key twice, hard. "We're in."

The three of us silently gathered behind him

while he searched through files. A half an hour later, we were shocked.

"Well, *that* changes things, doesn't it?" Pepper exhaled. "It doesn't make any sense. Why didn't he say anything?"

"Play it one more time?" I asked.

Ollie hit play, and the four of us watched Tom Wilson, a woman, and Bill Johnson pack backpacks full of shovels and pans. At one point, Tom went into the back in his mailman's uniform and emerged five minutes later dressed in hiking boots, denim jeans, and an army jacket.

I recognized the outfit.

It was the one he was wearing when he died.

The grainy video followed the three as they lugged the tools to the front door. An outside camera captured the group climbing into a car at the edge of the frame.

The timestamp was 8 p.m.

Just a few hours before we stumbled over Tom, dead.

FIFTEEN

When Gabe returned, Ollie reported what he'd discovered from his illegal hacking of Bill Johnson's *Rock Shop*. Despite not wanting to be there for the illicit act, the upstanding Detective Wilcox was *happy* to discuss the information gained, *and* view the stolen footage.

I watched the conversation silently, not alarmed, but not comfortable with the turn of events. Something about it felt wrong.

"Lines are never as black and white as you think they are, are they?" Martin asked me quietly, slipping into the chair next to me. I turned and looked over at him. He looked relieved...and tired. "You look troubled. Which is to be expected, I—"

"You know, I hid evidence a few months ago," I admitted, turning to face him. "It was manufactured, and it was planted, and it was put in my house as part of a frame job by a killer. But if you get down to brass tacks, I concealed evidence from the police. Which is illegal—even when the police are idiots."

"This bothers you."

"I thought it was necessary, but now I wonder. Does that make me a bad person?" I asked him. "Corrupt?" Without waiting for him to answer, I continued. "I know that Pepper does a whole host of things she shouldn't to get the information she wants to expose things she disagrees with. Illegal things. One of the first things we did after meeting was break into the cage to look at police records. With the town librarian's help, no less," I said with a snort.

"Are you having second thoughts about having done those things?"

"No, what I'm questioning is how I can do all those things—how we can do all those things—and still have any moral high ground to claim here. Technically, everyone in this room is a criminal in one way or another. Every person took part in a crime," I pointed out. Tilting my head, I studied him. "Well, except for you. As far as I know."

"Ironic, isn't it?" he smiled.

"Yeah, a little," I nodded.

Martin sat quietly watching me while Pepper, Ollie, and Gabe compared and contrasted the information they had seen, the information they had, and the information they needed to find.

"You *could* have talked to me, you know," I told him.

"As you could have to me," Martin said.

"Hey, I *did* talk to you, Martin," I told him, my anger flaring. "Well, I *tried*, at least. I called three times a day *for a week* and left messages that were never returned."

"You're right, you're right. I'm sorry that I was too much of a coward to return the call." He leaned away and drew his shoulders back. Gideon walked over and placed his head in Martin's lap, the hound's soft eyes looking up at the gangster's son warmly. Martin looked down, surprised, and caressed the dog's gray snout. "I didn't realize..."

Martin trailed off and said nothing more.

"Was it that you were the son of Marty Salvatore? The fact that I was a witch? The almost-shooting at the mansion? What *was* it, exactly, that made you ghost me like that?"

Martin continued petting Gideon, his full attention on the dog, for a minute more. Maybe two. I sensed chaos within him, a struggle over the next step.

I waited, not interfering. Hoping that my silence would get me the real answer, the complete response. *Finally.*

Or not.

"The idea of something happening to you, Fortuna, is almost unbearable to me," he said, his dark eyes locking on mine. "I didn't know it until I almost lost you that day at the funeral. It...surprised me. How worried I was. How...Anyway, I realized the two of us being near each other made that danger far more real."

"Why?"

Silence. I waited. *More* silence. He stared back at me, his handsome face blank as he hid again behind his mask.

Ugh. Why were mysterious men so maddening and sexy? It was *distracting*.

"Okay, why are you here now, then?" I asked him.

"In truth, part of me believes I shouldn't be," he responded.

"You are absolutely, unbelievably *infuriating*, Martin," I told him, breathing out forcefully with exasperation as I gave voice to my thought. "And incidentally, your Uncle Vito disagrees with you."

"I've told you as much as I can tell you for now," he said. He stopped petting Gideon and reached for my hand. "I'm hoping it's enough that we can begin to repair—"

"Yeah, well, it's *not*." I yanked my hand away and stood up to join the others. "I don't know whether to believe you, and that's because you're *not* telling me the full story."

"Fortuna—"

"Save it." I walked away. "I have a ghost to extract from a rock."

Gideon whined.

"You save it, too, dog."

* * *

"Now, no, move that clue over there," Pepper said, pointing to the video evidence.

"Oh, for heaven's sake." I jerked my hand and moved all the clues into a grid on the whiteboard, stars next to the important ones suggesting a suspect.

Gabe, Ollie, and Martin stared at me.

Pepper smirked at their gobsmacked expressions.

"Thank you," she nodded. "Your magic has much better handwriting than any of these guys."

"We're missing a huge piece of information, though," Pepper said, tapping an empty square.

"Who was Tom having an affair with? Did Emily know?"

"If she did, she didn't say, why don't we just—"

"Did you see anything at his apartment that might give us a clue?" Gabe asked Pepper. He examined the board and tilted his head. "A card, pictures, anything?"

Pepper shook her head.

"Guys, why don't we just—"

"Ollie, can you hack his email?" Pepper asked.

"Would you stop it?" I snapped with irritation, and all three stopped and turned their eyes wide. "My stars, you three are like psychotic kittens chasing a laser pointer *off a cliff!*"

"Hey, I didn't say anything," Ollie said, half-smirking. "Don't gripe at me for over-looking the obvious. *I* see the obvious. But this clearly ain't my rodeo."

"What do you mean?" Pepper asked.

I turned on my heel and went back to the front, picked up the smoky quartz, and brought it into the studio. I held it up and then placed it down on the center of the table with a thud. Holding up my phone, I turned the volume up with exaggerated motions and placed it next to the rock. Then I pointed.

"Just ask him," I said.

"Ow," the computer-formed voice said.

"Sorry," I told the rock.

"Oh, right," Gabe said, his face turning slightly pink.

"Look, it's not like we're *used* to this, okay?" Pepper told me in their defense. "Even after the whole magic book being vomited up by the earth thing, I still forget sometimes—"

"What's that now?" Gabe asked, looking back and forth between us.

"Never you mind, Detective. Ask Tom what you want to know," I repeated.

"So, um, Tom," Pepper said. She leaned down on the table and placed her face close to the sparkly rock. "Who were you cheating on your wife with?"

"Lulu."

"Lulu, the third person in your little threesome rock-hock agreement? That Lulu?

"Yes."

"Hey, Tom, how serious were you and Lulu?" I asked. We drew closer to the smoky quartz. Despite staring at it intently, it just looked like a big brown crystal rock. I mean, it was a *pretty* crystal as far as crystals go. But it also seemed pretty nondescript for a psychic prison. "Was this just a mid-life crisis fling or something more serious?"

"Fling. Serious."

"That was a one or the other question, Tom," Pepper warned the rock. "It *can't* be both, buddy."

The storefront's bells rang out, and I heard Jeeves tell whoever had entered that we were closed. Rolling my eyes, I turned away from the group.

"Where are you going?" Martin asked.

"I have a customer. Just give me a second."

It turned out I would need more than a second.

* * *

"Rick! What are you doing here?" "Do you have *any* idea the issues you caused with your fake psychic crap?" the usually mild-mannered nurse from Mystic Memories exploded at me, fists balled. "How could you *do* that to a grieving widow?"

"Rick, I—"

"She told her parents that Tom was *murdered!*" he shouted. "Then *her* parents called *his* parents, and they came over! Now they're *all* holding a seance trying to contact Tom to find out what happened to him like a bunch of *loons!*" He grabbed my arm so forcefully that I was sure his grip would be immortalized in purple for a few days.

"Rick, let go of me!"

Jeeves and Gideon both stormed toward him, teeth bared in a snarl. The bodyguard's approach was silent while the greyhound's advance was far more swift and loud, his angry bark echoing off the walls.

The dog reached Rick first and launched at him. The three of us crashed to the ground ungracefully with a thud and I felt claws rake across my torso. We all struggled against each other on the floor.

I had read in the greyhound book from the library that greyhounds made terrible guard dogs. They were conflict-averse, rarely barked, and exceptionally friendly.

Reconciling *that* description with *my* adorable, skinny hound was difficult with him snarling and roaring like an angry wolf.

Books and walls and dog limbs whizzed passed me while strong hands lifted me and carried me away from the chaos. I could hear the struggle behind me as whoever took me spirited me some distance away.

"Are you okay?" Martin placed my feet back on the floor.

"Yeah, so, this started out with the dude just grabbing my arm. Jeeves and Gideon made the situation a *little* more violent than it needed to be," I complained. I reached my hand out for the bookshelf and leaned over to catch my breath. My shirt was torn. "Darn it. I *love* this shirt."

"Are you *trying* to get arrested?" Gabriel asked Rick while Jeeves pinned his arms from behind.

"You people are crazy, all of you!" Rick jerked once, trying to get away from Martin's bodyguard. Jeeves barely flinched and did not release his hold. "Salvi, you better get this guy *off* me."

"Jeeves, let him go, please," I gasped.

Jeeves looked at Martin for the okay.

Martin didn't give it.

"What's he going to do, Martin? There are four people in here with the two of us. Five if you count the dog."

"I saw Gideon take that leap, I would *totally* count the dog," Pepper murmured, winking at the greyhound.

Gideon wagged his tail back and barked happily at her.

"Martin, tell your man to let him go," I snapped.

Martin nodded at Jeeves, who released Rick's arms. Rick jerked away dramatically and glared behind him.

"What are you *so* angry about?" I asked Rick. "That Tom's family is trying to contact him in the afterlife? Really?"

"I've been in love with that woman since high school!" Rick snapped. He rubbed his forearm—an action that made me feel satisfied, I must admit. I hoped his arm was *twice* as sore as mine was. "I wouldn't have wished that guy dead, not *ever*—but he is, except *you* convinced her that she can contact him!"

"Are you seriously complaining to me that my telling Emily a tidbit about her husband and how he died screwed up *your dating life*? Are you *that* much of a jerk?"

"It's more than that. She's not gonna let him go now!"

"He died, like, *yesterday*, dude!" Pepper told him incredulously. "You're not even going to wait until his body's in the ground?"

"It's not about that!" he roared. "I care about Emily, and she's *suffering*, and it's your fault! He didn't deserve her in life, and he doesn't deserve her feelings now!"

"She's suffering because her husband and the father of her unborn child *died*, you idiot," I snapped at him. "Are you *that* lacking in compassion? You work in a nursing home, for goodness sake! Never been around a grieving spouse before?"

"It's not about that! It's not about that! Why don't you understand? Tom Wilson *cheated* on Emily for the last two years with Lulu Miller. *Two years* he humiliated her! Two entire years he lied to her—"

"What do you mean he *lied* to her?" I asked

him, confused. "I talked to Emily myself this morning. She was aware that Tom had cheated on her."

"She wasn't aware that he got his mistress *pregnant*." Rick crossed his arms and glared at me. My jaw dropped. "You may need to shine up your crystal ball, there, fortune teller," he sneered. "You look a little surprised."

"What do you mean?" Pepper asked. "Lulu was pregnant?"

"*Is* pregnant," he corrected, his face showing his disgust. "Just about the same amount of pregnant as Emily, too."

"How do *you* know all this?" I asked Rick.

Rick shifted uncomfortably.

"Rick, how do you know that Lulu's pregnant?"

"She works for my dad's towing company," Rick said. In the middle of his statement, he looked away. It was shifty. Like he was hiding something.

"*And?*"

Rick glared at me.

"Should I break out the crystal ball?" I asked sarcastically.

"She's my half-sister," he grumbled.

"Wait, I know your parents," Gabe said, his face confused. "They've been married for fifty..." Gabe's eyes widened. "Oh. *Half*-sister."

Pepper gave a long, slow whistle. "I guess infidelity runs in the family."

"Rick, maybe you should calm down, sit down, and start at the top," I told him and gestured toward the back.

SIXTEEN

"We were all friends, more or less." Rick eyed the clue board. Spotting his name as a suspect, he frowned, but continued with his story without asking why he was listed up there. "Tom, Emily, me, Lulu. I didn't realize Lulu was my half-sister until about four years ago."

"How did you find out?" Pepper asked him.

"Dad hired her," Rick said. "I started to notice the likeness when they stood next to one another. I mean, I'd *known* Lulu for a few years socially, but since I never saw her standing next to Dad, I just never saw what was right in front of my face."

"But who confirmed it for you?" Pepper asked.

"Lulu," Rick said.

"That must've hurt, finding out your father cheated on your mother and kept your half-sister from you," I said.

"Not really," Rick shrugged. "Dad's never been faithful, and it's not like there was just *one* mistress, you know? My mom knew all about it. Okay, maybe not about Lulu."

"While all this is fascinating, I don't understand what it has to do with Tom. Does it?"

"Does it what?" Rick asked me, looking confused.

"Your family history of infidelity. What does *any* of this have to do with Tom and Lulu?"

"Nothing, really."

"Let's fast-forward, then, to the part that *does*."

"Spoilsport," Pepper told me.

"Look, all I want to do is get a man *out* of a rock. If we solve the murder in the process and unwind some mystery, great. But my *only* goal here is to get a man out of a rock."

"I don't understand," Rick frowned.

"You don't have to," I told him. "So, Lulu's pregnant. You know because you're her half-brother, and presumably, because the two of you have built up a relationship over the past few years. Yes?"

Rick blinked. Then his eyes narrowed. "Are you doing some psychic mumbo-jumbo reading on me?"

"Yes, it's called using my brain," I told him sarcastically. I had liked Rick until this week. I even thought about going out digging with him. He'd *seemed* like a kind, smart, and empathetic guy.

Seemingly, my dude radar was on the fritz.

"I don't want you to use any psychic stuff on me," Rick warned.

"Since you don't believe in it, I guess I can't use *any* of it on you, so you're good." Pepper and Gabe both pulled hands to their mouths to cover their quiet snorts of amusement. "Did your sister tell Tom that she was pregnant?"

"Yeah, she did, and *that jerk* told her that he only needed one child and couldn't support two on a mail carrier's salary," Rick told me angrily.

"*When* did she tell him?"

"I don't know," he shrugged. "I found out last night after I talked to Lulu. I mean, she only told me last night, but she didn't tell me when she told... him..." Rick stopped abruptly and scanned around the table. "Wait a minute. Why are you asking me all these questions?" He turned back and looked at the board again.

"We are trying to find out what happened to Tom," I told him, although the board should have made *that* darn obvious. "We're not sure it was an accident."

Rick stood up from the table and stepped back,

sliding the chair loudly across the floor. "You're *not* gonna pin this on Lulu!"

"We're not trying to *pin* this on anyone," Gabe told him. "This isn't an official police investigation. We're just curious about what happened."

"Right. That's why a detective is sitting at this table, right?" Rick demanded angrily. "And you," Rick turned to Ollie. "I know you. You work for the coroner's office!" Ollie's expression remained unchanged. "You take the old biddies from the nursing home all the time!"

"And me?"

"We *know* who you are, Pepper," Rick nodded curtly.

"It's so nice to be recognized for my achievements," Pepper beamed proudly. "So, since you know who *we* are, you should just answer our questions. We're *going* to figure out what happened, anyway. I mean, look at this group!" she told him, her arms wide.

"Oh yeah, what about *him?*" Rick asked Pepper, pointing at Martin.

"Funding for the investigation, obviously," Pepper spun on the spot.

"I contribute the armed security," Martin said in a low tone and pointed toward Jeeves. Jeeves stared back at Rick silently and opened his jacket to show the gun strapped to his side in a shoulder holster. "Jeeves, it's not concealed if you *show* them," Martin chided his body man.

"Apologies, sir," Jeeves nodded and closed his jacket.

"You people are *crazy*," Rick said to no one in particular. "You leave my sister alone, you hear me? She's been through *enough*. Just leave her alone."

"Calm down, Rick," Martin warned the man.

"Oh, screw *you*, rich man." The nurse flushed angrily, but he seemed to realize he had gone too far when Jeeves stepped toward him, the jacket fluttering menacingly. "Dude, just take a step back. I'm not going to *do* anything to anybody."

"Look, Rick, just answer me this one question. Can you answer *one* question for me?" I asked him, my voice calm and infallibly polite.

Rick's eyes turned cold, but he nodded once.

"Who else knew that Lulu and Tom were having an affair? And if you don't mind answering a second question, who else knew that she was pregnant?"

"I came over here to get you to leave Emily alone, and somehow you turned this all around on *me*," Rick complained and crossed his arms. I stared at him for a moment but didn't respond. I was afraid if I said anything else, he would find a reason to dig in and not answer.

Finally, he sighed.

"Look, *many* people knew about the two of them and the way they were carrying on. I'd be here all night if I tried to list them. About the baby? Hardly anyone, as far as I know. Lulu only found out last week."

"Do you know who those 'hardly anyone' people are?"

"Me," he said. "I know Lulu told Tom. I think she told him when they were both with Bill, so I'd guess he knows. The three of them were digging somewhere or something."

My ears perked up. "When was this?"

"I've answered *enough* of your questions. Leave Emily alone, Fortuna. No more of your psychic mumbo-jumbo," he warned me again and turned to leave. "I *mean* it. Let her heal and focus on her baby. Not that jerk of a husband she has to put in the ground."

"You're happy he's dead," Martin remarked.

"Damn *right*, I am," Rick answered without turning around. "Doesn't mean I killed him," he added, walking through the archway into the front of the store.

* * *

"I feel like we need to organize our questioning," Pepper said once the bell announced that Rick had left. "Oh, and could we *please* lock the door? Anyone could walk in off the street."

"That's the *point* of a store, Pepper. I want anyone to be able to walk in off the street. To *buy* things."

"It's already dark, just lock it. Okay, mailman." Pepper leaned in toward the rock. "I know we're sort of committed to helping you get out of the rock, but I'm starting to wonder if this whole *captured in a rock* thing isn't your karma, buddy."

"You do sound like a jerk," I added.

"Made. Mistakes."

"Well, *that's* the understatement of the year," Ollie noted. "Pepper, I thought you talked to the guy at the rock shop. That's Bill, right? The guy we hacked?"

"Yeah, I did."

"Rick said that Bill knows about Lulu's pregnancy." Ollie looked at her curiously. "But Bill didn't say anything to you at all about it. Not about that, and not about the three of them going to dig together the night that Tom was killed. Hey, Tom?"

"Yes."

"Who do you think killed you?" Ollie asked, his eyes alert.

"Wow," Pepper said. "Didn't we ask him?"

I shook my head no. "I don't think so. We asked him what he remembered, but not much more than that. It took him a while to get the hang of the app, though."

"Okay, I'm embarrassed." Pepper shifted uncomfortably. "I need to start integrating this otherworldly interview technique into my repertoire."

"No. One. People. Liked. Me."

"Dude, *you've* got some self-awareness issues," Pepper muttered and then cleared her throat. "Okay, let's say *everyone* liked you. On the day you died, who was the *angriest* at you even though they liked you?"

We paused, staring back and forth between the rock and the cell phone.

"Lulu."

"Pregnancy hormones," Pepper nodded as if she had solved the case. "I've heard that pregnancy hormones can be pretty gnarly. Like PMS on steroids."

"Tom, did you tell Lulu you were going back to Emily that night?"

"Yes."

"*Did* you tell her that you could only afford one child?" I asked him. Even if he *did* say it, it didn't mean that he was urging Lulu not to have the baby. He could have just been pointing out that his salary would make it difficult to raise two children. Maybe.

Even as I justified it, I knew I was trying to be generous.

Silence.

"So, you know, if a man said that to *me*? I'd think about killing him. I mean, I *probably* wouldn't, but the *urge* would sure be there," Pepper said, trying to hide a yawn behind her hand. "Man, we've been at this all day. Oh, and I don't know if any of you noticed this, but I realized something."

"What?" Gabe asked her without frowning, or a snarky look on his face, or angry judgment. I was impressed.

"When that rock came sailing through the front window? I heard chains," she said. "Loud, clanging chains."

"Me, too," I told her after thinking back.

"You know what has chains?"

"A tow truck," Ollie said, his eyes widening.

"And who just marched in *here* complaining about Fortuna's psychic whatever with Emily?"

"Lulu the tow truck driver's brother," Gabe said.

"You think he told her about this morning?" Pepper asked.

"But why would Lulu throw a rock through your window?" Martin asked, his face confused.

"Because Lulu killed Tom?" Pepper guessed.

"I mean, again, I have to point out that if a guy did to me what Tom did to Lulu? *I'd* want to kill him."

"Noted," Gabe said.

"What I mean is...look, there's a timeline starting to emerge, right?" Pepper pointed out. She walked over to the board, scribbled a few more points, and then poked each with her finger. "Emily tells Tom she's pregnant. Lulu tells Tom she's pregnant. Three people—Lulu, Bill, and Tom—gather supplies as if they're going into the forest to dig for rocks. Two hours later, Tom's dead. It seems *pretty* obvious to me."

"Tom *probably* told Lulu about Emily's pregnancy when they went out that night, and Lulu smashed him in the head with a rock." Gabe uncrossed his arms and stretched them above his head. "The only question is whether Bill knew or he left the forest before it happened."

"I think it's a theory," I said, suppressing the urge to roll my eyes at the immediate jumping to conclusions. "But Bill didn't even mention to Pepper that he had seen Tom that night—"

"Yeah, but I didn't *ask* him."

"You didn't ask when he saw the deceased last? Wouldn't that be, like, interrogation question number one?"

"Okay, I did ask *that*, but he said that *day*. He

didn't elaborate. So he didn't technically lie to me about the digging trip."

"But he didn't volunteer any information."

"*Or* contact the police to say he was in the forest the night Tom died," Gabe added.

"That doesn't seem so suspicious to me, though. Why would Bill bother contacting you?" I asked Gabe and then yawned. "You folks ruled it accidental."

The group fell silent, thinking.

"You know, it's been a long day," Pepper said finally. "How about we meet back here in the morning? We could all use some sleep."

"I'm game," Ollie nodded.

Everyone stood up and bade everyone else good night. Despite the anger and frustration of the past two months, everyone was polite, and it *seemed* the day's bonding had lowered some resentment among different members of the group.

"I'm leaving Jeeves here." Martin stepped forward as if he wanted to hug me, but wasn't sure that he should. "No arguments, Fortuna. I won't sleep tonight if I think you're here unprotected."

"I have magic, remember?"

"I prefer for you to have an armed guard as a backup to your magic," he countered. I didn't have the energy to argue with him, and I shrugged. "He'll be right outside."

"Sounds good."

"I'll be back in the morning. Is there anything, in particular, you would like for breakfast?"

I stared up at Martin, not sure what to say.

His act of bringing me food seemed like a threshold waiting to be crossed. It had been a facet of our relationship. An aspect integral to us getting to know one another—the absence of which had been a *clear* signal of a friendship broken.

"Just make sure you bring bacon for Gideon," I said finally, giving him implicit permission to take a small step back in my life. Gideon pressed against Martin's leg, barked, and wiggled happily.

"Absolutely," he nodded and reached out his hand to lightly touch my shoulder. It was as far as he would go, and I was grateful he didn't push further.

* * *

Later, I was in my bathroom, brushing my teeth, thinking about the day's events.

Relationships were so *complicated*.

I eyed the clawfoot tub while I brushed, and then dismissed the idea of a bath. I was weary, both from the mental effort of trying to figure out Tom Wilson's life and death, and the emotional struggle of trying to work out the complex dynamics of my newly formed friend group.

I climbed into bed without checking for Jeeves out the window. I knew he'd be there, on alert, all night. Gideon leapt onto the bed and snuggled up next to me. Soon, he was snoring, dreaming of restaurant-cooked bacon.

It was a long time before I finally drifted off to sleep.

SEVENTEEN

I awakened early, still tired.

Part of it was that I wanted to be dressed before Martin got to my place, and part of it was that Gideon wanted me out of bed because he knew Martin was coming.

With bacon.

The sun had just barely risen, and the light from the dawn sky cast a clean glow across my bedroom. I crawled out of bed, grabbed the robe that hung on my bedpost, walked toward the window and looked down, Jeeves looked up at me and gave me a quick, formal nod in greeting.

By everything I sensed, the man *seemed* human.

When the heck did the guy sleep?

I nodded back, and he looked away to resume scanning the street for threats.

"Why did I come here, Gideon, if all I was going to do was get involved in the same garbage that happened at the Magical Midway?" I asked the greyhound. Gideon looked up, still snuggled in bed. "You know, I came here to find out who my birth parents were, and I *haven't* done that."

An image of me holding my palms away from my body. Then a more forceful one of me turning my face to the side repeatedly. Miss Bessie appeared and disappeared in the vision.

"Yes, okay, I *could* have. I haven't, have I?" I asked the dog. "I don't even really know *why* I haven't gone to talk to her, Gideon. It just seems like other things keep taking priority."

An image of the dog holding up an animated sign flashed in my mind. On the sign was a plate of bacon and a little stick figure puppy trying to grab it. Every time he got close, the puppy changed his mind and pushed the plate of bacon away.

"I don't understand what you're trying to tell me," I frowned.

"You. Get. Close. You. Push. Truth. Away," the phone boomed. "You. Do. Not. Want. Two. No."

"Good morning, Tom," I told the smoky quartz. "I don't know that it's as simple as all that. There's been a lot going on in the few months since I moved to Mystic's End, you know. Hey, by the way, can you see out of that rock?" I asked him while I pulled clothes from my closet for the day.

"No. Sea," he answered.

"Considering all we learned about you last night, buddy, I'm not sure I *believe* you," I muttered while I pulled out a tee shirt. Turning, I grabbed a pillow from my bed and tossed it onto the smoky quartz. "If you can't see, that shouldn't be a problem, then."

"Dog. Think. You. Push. Truth. Away."

"I don't know that I'm *pushing* the truth away," I said as I undressed. "*Avoiding* the truth? Maybe. But if it was right in front of me, I don't think I would *actively* turn away from it."

"Would," the phone disagreed.

"You *don't* know me. Heck, it doesn't seem like you knew *yourself* all that well," I told the ghost in the rock. I slipped my shirt over my head. "Look, I came here to get the truth, that's true. And I haven't been as diligent in trying to uncover it as I *could* have been."

"Ignore. Be. Sea."

"Bessie?"

"Yes."

"That was more out of respect for Gabe," I told Tom and I pulled my jeans on. "He was pretty angry."

"Con. Vein. Went. Ex. Queues."

"If that was your take at a snarky comeback of *convenient excuse*, sure, I'll agree with you." I jumped once and snapped my jeans. "Nevertheless, it didn't completely stem from my need to avoid the truth about myself."

"Not. Ready," Tom said after a while.

I didn't know whether that was Tom's observation or Gideon's observation, but either way, it was right. I didn't understand why I wasn't ready, though, or why I had been so excited to move here only to be frozen with indecision once I arrived. Well, not *frozen* with indecision. Just no longer... feeling urgency.

My lack of a birth story had always been a hole. I had to navigate *around* that hole for as long as I could remember. It was a hole, though, that was *part* of me. I didn't know what would fill it, or how that new knowledge would change me.

"I'm allowed not to be ready, you know," I told Gideon, or Tom, or both. "Maybe I don't have to know. Maybe the idea that I need to know where I came from isn't right. Maybe that's not what I'm doing here at all."

"Why," the phone asked.

"Maybe I don't want anyone to tell me who I am anymore," I told them, standing up straight. "Maybe coming here to find my birth story was just another way of avoiding responsibility for deciding who I am. Choosing where I fit. On my terms and no one else's."

"Lot. Of. Maybe."

Gideon sent me an image of myself flexing biceps I didn't have.

"Thanks, Gideon," I told the dog. I scratched him vigorously. My hand was mid-scratch when the bell rang. Gideon launched himself off the bed and scrambled down the stairs. Visions of bacon danced in his head. I scooped up the quartz and followed.

* * *

"You're up early," I said, letting Martin in. He carried two bags, one marked Gideon, and one marked Fortuna. If the one marked Gideon was filled with bacon? I would be cleaning up dog vomit *all* day.

"I wanted to get here before the others, and I wasn't sure when they would arrive," Martin said, waiting at the base of the stairs for me to start up. I didn't know if it was due to politeness or discomfort that he waited for me to go first.

"Pepper doesn't get out of bed before nine unless Jason Momoa is *in* her bedroom to wake her," I gestured toward a stool and hit the button on the coffee pot. "I take it this is Gideon's bacon?"

"I brought enough for a few days," Martin nodded and looked behind him. The greyhound was sitting at attention, staring at Martin as if Martin himself was a slice of bacon. Drool dripped from the dog's mouth, and he panted as if he had just run a race.

"Does this need to be warmed up?" I grabbed the other bag.

"It's up to you."

I unpacked the bag to find a stunning breakfast, fancier than any breakfast I had ever seen before. "So, that's an egg," I pointed. "And that *looks* like a berry. And that's a mushroom, right? Or, wait, no," I stared and then looked up at him. "I give up. I have *no* idea what this is."

"Pan poached egg with hazelnuts, chanterelles, green garlic, and blackberries."

"Chanterelles. Mushrooms?" I pointed.

"It's a type, yes," he laughed.

"I've never seen them before."

"They are a delicacy."

"You mean expensive."

"Two hundred twenty-four dollars a pound and worth *every* penny." Martin smiled, grabbed the takeout container from me, and walked over to where I kept the plates. "It's a decadent experience, these mushrooms, I promise. They have a woodsy, earthy flavor."

"Don't *all* mushrooms have a woodsy, earthy flavor since they grow in the dirt in the woods?" I asked him as he plated the meals.

Martin smiled and passed my plate. "I thought you grew up as a young woman of means, Ms. Delphi. I'm shocked that your family never introduced you to these mushrooms," Martin said, sitting down with his own plate of obscenely priced fungus.

"My mother was *not* a fan of mushrooms," I told him and I tasted the incredible breakfast he brought me. "And whatever Mother was not a fan of did not get past the front door of her house. The servants would never have brought a mushroom within an acre of the house. Heck, I think the gardeners probably hand yanked and burned them if they were anywhere on the grounds."

"That's an intense dislike of mushrooms," Martin noted and then took another bite.

"Yeah, not a fan is putting it mildly."

Gideon whined, and I jumped to get the patient greyhound his promised bacon.

"She's getting it," Martin told the hopping greyhound. "Just take a breath, speedy."

Once I placed the plate on the floor, Gideon attacked it.

"Back to my bourgeois mushrooms," I said, sitting back down next to Martin.

"I'm glad you're enjoying them, *even* if you feel the need to insult them," Martin smiled at me.

"I swore I wouldn't engage in this kind of extravagance when I left my parents," I told him, waving my fork over the plate.

"Like fifty thousand dollar dogs?"

"Har har. That was different. Anyway, I realized that a wholesale rejection of everything I grew up with? That gives them just as much control over me the same as if I did everything they want me to, you know?"

"Difficult trying to strike that balance, isn't it?"

"Not as hard when you don't speak to them," I admitted.

"You don't talk to your parents anymore? Either of them?"

I looked down at my plate and tried to decide how much I wanted to share. On the one hand, Martin and I nearly destroyed our friendship by keeping secrets. But one breakfast over upscale mushrooms did *not* repair two months of anger.

"How about we not delve into our parents for a bit and talk instead about why you disappeared?" I said, changing the subject. "I don't want to give you the wrong impression here. I may have forgiven you for the past two months, but I still don't know why you did it, and I *haven't* forgotten that you did."

"Since it was just a few days ago, I didn't

suppose you would have." Martin pushed his plate away.

"Don't you *dare* waste those mushrooms. That's an extravagant expense if you eat them, and it's a *patently obscene* waste if you don't," I told Martin, pointing my fork toward his plate. "I will lose all respect for you if the food on the plate goes in the trash."

"Do you have any respect left for me that I can lose?" Martin asked uncomfortably. He fidgeted in his seat and then turned toward me, his eyebrow raised.

I stared back at him. "You really want the truth?"

He nodded.

"I don't know," I said with as much seriousness as I could muster. "I don't know if I respect you. I know for *sure* that I don't trust you. Right now, I'm willing to try and be your friend. And see if you're capable of being mine."

"Capable?"

"Look, Martin," I said, turning toward him. "You've made no secret of your feelings for me. Well, at least when we are speaking to each other. It's clear you want more than a friendship, and right now I'm still trying to decide *whether* I want to be your friend, and how much of a friend I want to be."

"I see," he responded softly.

"I'm *not* your girlfriend." I stood up and poured myself another coffee. "After what happened in the past two months? I don't know if something like that is even a possibility anymore. I'm adopted. I don't know if you know what that means, but people abandoning me? That's a *big* thing for me."

"It was never my intent—"

My glare of fury stopped him.

"You know, I just realized I *no longer care* what your goal was," I said. "I've asked you more than enough times *why* you did what you did. You've chosen for whatever reason not to tell me. *You've* set the ground rules here. I am not going to beg for answers I'm entitled to. It's humiliating, and I won't do it anymore. I'm *done*. You have a second chance, but you're starting further back than you did originally. Cards on the table."

I could see that statement had some impact, but what effect, I couldn't tell.

"And let's remember I *still* have an issue with the fact that you make your living exploiting dogs," I pointed out. "That was a problem for me *before* any of the rest of this happened."

"I made a mess of things, didn't I?" Martin said. He twisted himself away from me and rubbed his eyes with his hand. "I thought I was doing the right thing. I have to admit, I still think it would be better if I wasn't around you."

"Then *why* are you here?" I asked him with exasperation.

"There's something about you, Fortuna," Martin half-smiled. "I just like you. A lot. I'm drawn to you. I want to protect you."

It was like I was stuck in some terrible romantic movie where the ending was never *ever* going to be good.

"You're starting to sound all controlling and possessive again. I have to tell you, Martin, you're even less entitled to that attitude *now* than you were two months ago."

"I know," he nodded sadly and looked down.

"Look, this is how I feel right now." I leaned back on the counter and held up my hand. "Things *can* change, Martin. My feelings can change, *you* can change what you're hiding from me. I'm not saying *never*. I am saying that my not saying never *now* has a *much* longer runway than it did two months ago."

"Understood," he said.

"I welcome you back into my circle *as a friend*. But *just* a friend, Martin," I warned him, pointing my finger. "Before I would ever consider going out with you, you need to prove to me that I can trust you as a friend. And you have a way to go before you do that."

"Understood."

"And this puts me under *no obligation* for anything beyond friendship. Right?"

"Of course."

Martin smiled the broadest, most disarming smile I'd seen on his face in months.

I sighed.

While I was sure he *heard* what I said, I didn't know whether a man like him could respect *any* of it.

EIGHTEEN

"Before we get started, I want to make one thing clear to everybody," I said, giving Pepper a pointed glance as she kept talking. Once she quieted, I continued. "I know that you have jobs that let you walk away from them periodically, and while that's great for you, *I* have to leave the front door open. This is a business, and I have customers."

"Yeah, not that *many*, though, right?" Pepper said. "I mean, you were gone almost the whole day yesterday."

"And I may have missed customers."

"Do you have any classes today, Fortuna?" Gabe asked, a concerned look on his face.

"No."

"Well, I don't see any reason to hide what we're looking into. It's not a secret, is it?" Gabe asked me and then looked around the group. "Does anyone want to keep their involvement in this little group secret for some reason?"

"Well, I prefer that Bill and Lulu not be invited," Ollie pointed out. "Other than that, I don't care. It's all going to come out once we figure out who did this, anyway."

"Your confidence is inspiring," Pepper told Ollie cheerfully.

"I'm an inspiring kind of guy," Ollie responded cheerfully. He cocked his head. Then he winked at her. She giggled and blushed.

Were the two of them *flirting* with each other? I looked back and forth between them. Then I turned and glanced at Gabe, but he didn't seem bothered by their playful banter.

I tried to refocus on the matter at hand, even though what I *really* wanted to do was yank Pepper into another room and ask *what the heck* that was all about.

"Great, now that everyone's inspired, what do we think the next steps are?" I asked. "I think I should go talk to Bill at the rock shop and see if he tells me the same story he told Pepper yesterday."

"That's probably a good idea," Gabe nodded. "If he hasn't talked to Emily at all, he won't see you

coming. You can bring *moneybucks* over there."
Gabe pointed toward Martin. "Gush over the mega-
crystal and pretend you want to buy it. See if he's
willing to sell it to you. Martin's presence will make
it much more tempting an offer since he's cash-
rich."

"That's not a bad idea, Gabe," Pepper said,
looking at Gabe, her expression impressed. "We'll
make a detective of you yet."

"I have my moments," Gabe smiled back at her
and winked.

Pepper just made a sarcastic comment about
Gabe's detective skills, and Gabe didn't take offense
to it. *What* was going on here? Was everyone on
their way to getting along? Being *friendly*?

"I'd be happy to escort Fortuna to the rock shop
if you think it would help," Martin nodded, leaning
forward. "I don't know this Lulu person, so I can't
help there."

"Nobody has to know Lulu," Ollie told Martin.
"Somebody just needs a car without a distributor
cap so we can call a tow truck."

"Can we confirm she's working today?"

"Are we making this more complicated than it
needs to be?" I asked the group and looked at Gabe.
"Couldn't you go interview her about the rock
thrown through my window? We *heard* chains. Isn't
that enough to go talk to her?"

Gabe leaned back and thought a minute. "Maybe. It's not like I need a search warrant or anything."

"I saw her tow truck," Pepper told Gabe, nodding. "I saw it driving away after the window was shattered. Clear as day."

"You did?" Gabe asked, surprised. "Why didn't you say anything?"

"I just *did*."

"What did it look like?"

"A tow truck."

Gabe's eyes narrowed. "Describe it."

"It looked like a tow truck," Pepper repeated. "There. Go talk to her about the rock thrown through the window, and let her know that *someone* saw her driving away."

"Did you?"

"Am I going to have to swear an affidavit to it or testify under oath for you to go question her?" she asked.

"No."

"Well, then I absolutely, positively, *without a doubt* saw Lulu Miller driving her tow truck away from the scene of the crime," Pepper responded, nodding. "Not a question in my mind about what I saw."

"Not a doubt in my mind you're lying through your teeth," Gabe told her.

"Wow," she said, her eyes wide. "Detective, I'm *shocked* at your suggestion that I would make up such a thing. *You* need to investigate that."

"You know, lying to the police *is* a crime, right?" Ollie asked Pepper from across the table, his eyes glittering with amusement.

"I'm not filing a report," she argued.

"*Any* communication, either written or oral. Sworn *or* unsworn," Ollie told her.

"Well, shoot, then you need to arrest half the town," Pepper laughed.

"Pepper—"

"I wasn't talking to you or Gabe. I was talking to *her*." Pepper cut Ollie off and pointed her finger toward me. "You and Gabe just happened to overhear it. I didn't make any report to the police. Not *my* fault I'm loud."

"You are quick," Martin said with some admiration.

"I have *my* moments," Pepper winked at him and smiled at Gabe. "Are we set then, or do you need me to tell Fortuna something else?"

* * *

As Martin and I entered the rock shop, I gasped. The store was filled with shelf after shelf after shelf of multicolored crystals. There were spheres and towers in small clusters. A quiet, peaceful meditative chime rolled out of the speakers and over me.

The view of this place through the hacked video didn't do it justice. It was the most peaceful, most serene room I had *ever* stepped into. Turning to Martin, I could see from his expression that he, too, was affected.

"What can I help you two with?" A southern drawl boomed from the back. I turned and spotted a big, burly man with glasses and a shock of gray hair. The man's thick, hairy arms were smeared with dirt, as were his coveralls.

"Martin here promised me that he would buy me the biggest, best crystal in *all* of Mystic's End," I told Bill Johnson. I walked toward the glass-encased crystals in the back. "I want to see your biggest, best, *most extravagant* Arkansas crystal, sir. And *don't* you haggle," I told Martin with a frown. "It's bad luck."

"Well, now, miss, this here's the largest crystal we have." He came out from behind the counter and walked to a large display case containing Tom Wilson's once-in-a-lifetime find. "But it's not for sale."

"Surely *anything* is for sale for the right price," Martin told the older man knowingly. Bill glared at him, but then his jaw dropped.

"Mr. Salvi, sir," Bill coughed, his cheeks turning red. "I must need new glasses, I didn't recognize you with the girl," he said (while I gritted my teeth at being called a *girl*). "I'm sure that for you, that's true, but unfortunately this here crystal's not mine to sell. Belongs to a friend of mine."

"Well, give us his name, and we'll contact him," Martin told Bill. "I'm sure he'd be willing to hear our offer."

"Oh, I don't know that would be true *today*." Bill took a bandana out of his pocket and mopped his forehead. "She's going through some things, poor dear. Man she loved more than life itself died just a few days ago. *That* man, in fact." Bill nodded toward a framed article hanging to the right of the mega-crystal.

Her. Emily or Lulu?

"I think I read something in the newspaper about that," Martin nodded, stepping forward to skim. "He looks like he was a young man. This is the guy that tripped and fell?"

"Yes, sir, *tragic* fall in the forest. Rock diggers, we are a strange breed." Bill nodded and mopped his forehead again. "Don't know *what* Tom was thinking of, heading out at night by himself to look for rocks, but there you go."

"He went out to the forest alone?" I asked Bill.

"Yes, ma'am, according to the papers."

What about according to your discussions with him here, in this very room, the night he died? I wanted to ask it, but I *didn't* want to tip my hand just yet.

"Did you know him?" I asked instead.

I didn't know whether the ample amount of sweat beading along the forehead of the older man was due to discomfort about the mega-crystal discussion, or if the heavyset man just sweated a lot. What I *did* know was my question shocked him into immobility for a split second, and a flash of anger stabbed from him toward me.

"For many years, ma'am," he said slowly and turned away.

Martin glanced at me. "We're sorry for the loss of your friend."

Bill's neck tensed at Martin's apology.

"Yeah, well, everyone has to go at *some* point," the man responded gruffly. "Besides, I wouldn't *precisely* call me and Tom friends. Oh, I may have thought that *once*," he said, glaring at the quarter-million-dollar crystal display. "But no, in the end, me and Tom were definitely *not* friends."

"Did you two have a falling out?" I probed.

"You could say that," Bill said without turning around. "Yes, ma'am. I suppose you could say that." Then the man fell silent.

I shifted gears. Bill was clearly not going to talk

about the issue between him and Tom with two strangers that walked in off the street. Even if one stranger was the great Martin Salvi.

"So who owns this mega-crystal now?" I asked.

"The woman he was going to spend the rest of his life with." Bill turned toward me. "But like I said, ma'am, I don't think she'd want to negotiate the sale right now. She's upset that he is gone."

I nodded, then turned away.

It *sounded* like Bill was talking about Emily.

But I had to be sure, and questioning the man was like pulling teeth.

I leaned forward and looked at the pricier gems housed in a glass case and wrestled with my conscience. I *could* poke his head just a *little* bit. Just enough to know whether he was talking about Emily or Lulu.

It would violate the rules I had oathed to follow.

But it *would* get me an answer I needed.

No. I had some information already. We now knew Bill and Tom had some falling out after they left this place and before Tom died. That would *have* to do, right?

Even though that wasn't much. We knew walking in here things probably came down to Lulu or Bill.

Or Lulu *and* Bill.

All I knew now was not to discount Bill so easily.

I sighed.

"What's wrong?" Martin whispered over my shoulder and pretended to look at the gems while the suspect stacked boxes on the other side of the store.

"I'm trying to decide if I'm corrupt," I whispered back.

Martin looked surprised. "Are you doing it for a good reason?"

"Is doing a wrong thing *ever* justifiable?"

"Well, I guess that's the first thing you have to answer." Martin cast a sympathetic smile at me, and I sighed again. At least I was with Martin and not Pepper. Pepper probably would've gleefully enjoyed my discomfort.

I looked up at Bill, halfway across the room. What right did I have to go into his head and yank out what I wanted to know?

This happened for a reason, I heard Charlotte say in my head, a memory from one of our late-night conversations about witch powers. *If I can do these things, if I can make things better for people, don't I have a responsibility to do just that?*

Priestess Goodfellow tried to teach me human witch ethics.

But I wasn't a human witch.

"What were *you* doing the night that your friend was in the forest, Mr. Williams?" I asked. When the older man turned around and met my eyes, I reached in and captured the image in his mind.

"I was home," he lied.

* * *

"I don't know if I should have done that," I told Martin while Jeeves drove us back to my shop. "But I don't know that I *shouldn't* have."

"Deciding on your own morality is never easy," Martin responded, shifting across from me in the limousine. "I grew up knowing the ethical rules inside and out. And even though my family—some of them—are criminals, our family has a code. And *some* parts of it I, without a doubt, will follow until the day I die."

"I just feel like I keep trying to fit in *something*," I told him. "First, it was my adopted family, and then the Magical Midway. Then I was made a witch, and it was the witch world. Then I met Priestess Goodfellow, and I adopted the *human* witch rules," I explained. "On the one hand, I feel like I've learned a lot. On the other—"

"You feel like you keep throwing yourself into a

set of rules *someone else* came up with," Martin guessed.

"Exactly," I nodded. "But, in *this* town? No one follows the rules. I mean, no one. The police don't, prosecutors don't, the townsfolk, the church. All these written and unwritten rules? Everyone seems to spend all their time trying to figure out how to get *around* them."

"Okay, *that's* a little dark," Martin said, tilting his head. "Anyway, ethics and morals are *not* the same, Fortuna."

I frowned. "What do you mean? Of course they are."

"No, they're not." He shook his head. "Ethics are rules provided by an *external* source—like a code of conduct or a set of principles. Morals? Morals are *your own* set of principles about right and wrong."

"You sound like a philosophy major."

"Minor," he laughed. "Look, it sounds to me like your struggle is between ethics and morals. You've been searching for a set of ethics that fit you, and they keep coming up short. What you should be doing is deciding on your personal moral compass of right and wrong. If you can do that, do you *need* a set of ethics written by someone else to tell you what to do?"

"I never thought of it that way," I mused.

"Someone following strictly ethical principles may not have *any* morals at all," Martin said. "A moral person, on the other hand? They can choose to follow a code of ethics *if* it fits with their moral compass. Or not."

"So you're saying I have no moral compass," I responded wryly.

"I'm saying that you've spent *so* much time trying to find a set of ethics that fit you that you've neglected to shine up your own moral compass," Martin said. He hesitated a moment as if he wasn't sure whether to go on.

"What?"

"Or you haven't had the confidence in yourself to believe you have the right or the ability to make your own decisions about your own morality."

"*Ow*," I told him, wincing. "What did you major in, psychology?"

"Business," he said, shaking his head. "But I *do* know something about having the confidence to go your own way. I *can* tell you it's not easy."

"Is it worth it?" I asked him.

He paused, and turned to meet my eyes. "I'll let you know when I find out."

NINETEEN

"So, I sold some paint and stuff," Ollie said when Martin and I walked back into my shop. "The guy knew what he needed, and the register wasn't that hard to work."

"Thanks so much," I said gratefully. Gideon barked.

"How did it go at the rock shop?" Ollie asked.

"Bill did not want to sell us the mega-crystal," Martin told Ollie. "And he did recognize me *and* my deep pockets as we hoped." Martin smiled. "He was insistent it belonged to Tom's partner, but he didn't name names, so it was hard to figure out who he was referring to." Martin looked at me.

"That's too bad."

"He was talking about Lulu," I said. I felt

embarrassed at having to admit that I scooped the knowledge out of Bill's head. Even though I *did* it, I wasn't comfortable with my actions. Not yet.

"How do you know he was talking about Lulu and not Emily?" Ollie asked.

"She read his mind," Martin told him.

Ollie looked at me, his eyes wide with shock. "I thought you didn't do that," he said slowly.

"It's something I've done before," I shrugged, turning away from him and heading toward the counter to double-check the cash register. Not that I didn't trust Ollie. I just needed something to fiddle with so I wouldn't have to look him in the eye.

"Yeah, but I thought it was something you decided not to do anymore."

"Leaf. Fort. Tuna. Alone," the phone said, though it was muffled slightly by my purse.

"Fort Tuna? Seriously? Anyway, you were quiet back at Bill's," I told Tom. I pulled out the phone and put it on the counter.

"You. Took. Phone."

"I did," I told him.

"You. Left. Me."

"Oh, right," I blew out a breath and passed my hand in front of my eyes in embarrassment. "Limited distance and all that. Sorry. So, Bill told us the rock belongs to the woman you were going to spend the rest of your life with."

"Emily."

"Only *he* thought that was Lulu," I disagreed.

"Not. Likely."

"Did Lulu and Bill go out with you to the forest that night?"

"Think. Sew."

"Remember, Fortuna, he just passed away." Ollie leaned back and slipped his long brown hair behind him. "His memories of that day may not be clear. I wouldn't rely on him."

"I can't rely on anyone," I pointed out, worry creasing my brow. "Bill was hiding something, Tom doesn't remember and what he *does* remember he has difficulty communicating. I feel like I might accomplish more trying to pry open that book again and see if there's a spell just to yank him out."

"What book?" Martin asked. I didn't answer.

"Maybe Gabe and Pepper are getting better information," Ollie shrugged.

"Did they go and do the tow truck thing together?" I asked.

"Pepper went on her own, but I think Gabe's watching from down the street just in case," Ollie said.

"Does *she* know that?" I asked.

Ollie shrugged.

"Hey, *what* was that flirty banter thing between you and Pepper?" I asked him, thinking back to the two making eyes at each other. "I thought Gabe and Pepper were destined to be together. Or at least destined to pine over their relationship so they can't have a healthy one with anyone else."

"I would never ask Pepper out without Gabe's blessing," Ollie frowned and crossed his arms over his chest. "I know you don't know me that well, Fortuna, but Gabe and I have known each other for a *long* time. I'd never do anything to hurt them."

"Would that hurt him?" Martin asked, curious.

"I don't know," Ollie shrugged. "The two of them *do* love each other. I know that. Are they still *in love* with each other? I don't know." He smiled. "I don't even know if *they* know. They're like family, *that* I can tell you. Brother and sister or husband and wife? Don't know. Don't know if they know."

"Sorry, this is none of my business," Martin apologized as if he provoked more information than he felt he should know.

"Eh, it's just a question. Don't worry about it," Ollie said in his casual, friendly way. "I don't get too wrapped up in things, you know? Things will work out however they're going to work out."

"Well, I hope this Tom Wilson thing works out soon," I told Ollie. "He's murder on my phone's battery life." I grabbed the phone and plugged it in.

"I also don't know what it's like as a ghost to live in a crystal, but I *can't* believe it's comfortable."

"Is. Not," the phone interjected.

* * *

"Is Pepper back yet?" Gabe walked in just as Martin, Ollie, and I were finishing lunch.

"No, we thought she was with you," Martin said.

Gabe frowned.

"Lulu came by and didn't have to tow her anywhere, just gave her car a jump." Gabe pulled out a chair and sat down. He grabbed a carrot off the vegetable plate in the center of the table and bit it loudly. "We decided to replace her battery with a dead one since it was easier. So Lulu gave her a jump, they talked for a bit, and she drove away."

"Lulu or Pepper?" Ollie asked.

"Well, both," Gabe said, reaching for another carrot. "One went one way, and the other went another way." He frowned again. "We agreed to head back here as soon as it was over. She should've been here before me."

A faint, nervous flutter started in my stomach, a prickling sensation that made me feel slightly nauseous. I stood up abruptly and walked over to my phone to call Pepper.

The call went to voicemail.

"What is it?" Martin asked.

I hit her name on my contacts list again. The phone rang, and her voicemail picked up. I jabbed to hang up the call.

"Something's wrong," I told the men gathered around my table.

"Fortuna, Gabe *just* walked in the door," Martin said, frowning. "Maybe she stopped to get gas or to grab a sandwich. It is lunchtime. Give her a few more minutes."

I reluctantly sat down at the table, frequently glancing toward the front and back doors. My fingers drummed the table impatiently until Martin reached over and placed his hand on top of mine.

"Pepper can take care of herself," Martin told me softly.

"*Everyone* can take care of themselves right up until the point they can't," I told him. "Something's wrong," I repeated more insistently as the fluttering in my stomach grew steadily more persistent. "I just *know* it. Even if Pepper couldn't pick up the phone, she would text me back."

Thunder crashed outside as if to punctuate my anxiety, and Gideon jumped to his feet. Ollie and Gabe looked at one another as Martin continued staring at me with concern.

"Maybe she was driving," Martin suggested.

I glared at him.

"Okay, what do *you* think it is, Fortuna?" Gabe asked quietly.

"I don't *know*," I told him, shaking my head. I placed my hands on the area below my rib cage and pressed. "I don't know, it's just a feeling. My stomach is jumping like I'm on a roller coaster. I just know *something's* wrong."

"Jeeves," Martin barked over his shoulder at his body man. "Call our security and ask for them to be on the lookout for Pepper. You have her description? Her car?" he asked. Jeeves nodded silently. "Not just the security on the compound, either. The...the others, too—and have them check the cameras. All of them." Jeeves nodded again, turned on his heel, and walked toward the front of the shop.

"The *others*?" Gabe asked, his eyebrow raised.

"Do we want to have this discussion now?" Martin shot back.

"Just when I think I can *mostly* trust you, you say something that makes me wonder whether you've ever been honest with me," Gabe told him.

"At the end of the day, Detective, you are who you are, and I am who I am." Martin sat up and pulled his shoulders back. "Be grateful I have resources at my disposal to help look for Pepper, ones that won't raise eyebrows back at your station," he said.

"Gratitude *wasn't* the first emotion it crossed my mind to feel, *Mr. Salvi*," Gabe told Martin, shifting back to the more formal address while studying the wealthy man with suspicion. "But you're right, we can deal with this later. After we find Pepper."

I stared at Martin, uncomfortable again.

Then a wave of nausea hit me, and I threw up my lunch on the wealthy man's lap.

* * *

I lay in my bed alone.

The echoes of the men talking down below drifted faintly up the stairs. Gabe and Martin were arguing. Ollie jumped in periodically, trying to ratchet down the anger between them.

"Pepper, where *are* you?" I whispered. Another wave of nausea hit me even though I was lying down. But no image of her, no hint of where she could be. No picture, no flash.

Nothing.

I was out of practice using my powers. I had spent so much time tamping *down* my abilities and locking them away that now when I *desperately* needed them? They weren't so easy to call up anymore.

"Pepper, come on," I whispered to the empty room. "*Tell* me where you are. Tell me what's happening to you."

I closed my eyes and tried to open the box I had locked my abilities in, and reached out in all directions looking for Pepper's energy. It was a struggle—as if those senses had become used to being tied in knots and shoved down. Atrophied.

Pain shot through my body as I tried to awaken *myself*.

"Fortuna?" Spike whispered as his ghostly glow appeared in the darkened room. "Fortuna, what's going on? Are you okay?"

"I think something happened to Pepper," I whispered back, hoping to avoid the cavalry rushing up the stairs. "My abilities...I've ignored them and held them so rigidly in check for *so* many months that now when I need them, I *really* need them, I can't...I *can't* find her, Spike. I can't even figure out what's going on. If anything."

Spike floated to the bed next to me and hovered over the mattress. I was shocked that his Mohawk was gone, and his ghostly clothing was relatively conservative considering the full punk regalia I met him in. He looked like a stylish Brooklyn hipster.

"You look so different," I whispered, sitting up.

"Liz helped me find a style," he said, half smiling. "I was hoping to show you what I could do now."

"She helped you do this just talking to you through the app?" I whispered, surprised.

"Not entirely," he shrugged. "Liz talks to me a lot now that she knows I can hear her—even if I can't talk back as much. We talked about her struggles to get school paid, to come out to her parents as gay. I think it's just helped her to have someone to talk to," he smiled. "Hearing her stories? I guess she gave me the strength to try and see what I could do," he shrugged. "I mean, I didn't really *do* anything like a ghost because...Well, all those years, I was alone, right?"

I nodded.

"I'm not alone anymore," he shrugged again. "I may be dead, but I *can* have a life, you know? I don't want to be a pissed-off punk for the rest of my death. Anyway, I just started trying things," he smiled.

"You think it's easier to change when you have motivation to change, huh?" I whispered.

"I think it's easier to change when we accept who we are." Spike reached out with his ghost hand and tapped my forehead with his index finger. "I died, but I never *accepted* I was dead, I don't think." Spike paused and looked at me, tilting his head.

"You know, you became a witch, but you never really *accepted* you were. That you weren't human. Maybe if you *did*, Pepper would be easier to find."

"That sounds like something I would need years of therapy to do, Spike." I crossed my arms. "Not something that can be done in an afternoon."

"Bull. You're *magic*, Fortuna," Spike said, tilting his head. "Maybe for a human, it would take years of therapy. For you? I don't even think you'd need the afternoon."

As Spike spoke, he glowed in a kaleidoscope of colors. Hues of green, blue, and pink sparkled when he smiled.

"Just *take* the leap, friend," the ghost said.

I closed my eyes and pushed hard.

When I opened them, I was looking out over Mystic's End, through the solid walls of my home with eyes that could see to the psychic fence at the edge of town. "Oh my *gosh*," I whispered and looked down at my body. It still lay quietly on the bed, my eyes closed.

I looked back up and scanned the horizon.

"There!" I shouted. A shining light flashed from the direction of the forest, and I felt a jolt yank me back into my body.

TWENTY

"I didn't think I could fit this many people in here comfortably," Martin murmured, looking around at the group piled into the back of his limo. "I rarely have more than one or two."

"If I were camping, I could *live* in this thing comfortably for a month," Gabe told the gangster heir while peering out the window. "How much room do you need that you didn't think you could fit four people back here?"

"And the dog," Martin pointed toward Gideon. "That's five."

There were actually *six* people sitting comfortably. Spike sat on the floor between Martin, Gabe, Ollie, and myself, but no one else in the back of the limousine could see him. Jeeves steered the car through sheets of rain and a howling wind.

"Are you still feeling sick?" Martin asked me.

"The nauseous feeling went away once I used my powers to locate Pepper." I jumped when the thunderstorm cracked above our heads like a baseball bat, the sky glowering angrily through the falling rain.

"Wicked storm," Gabe said nervously. "Not sure the forest is the safest place at the moment."

"It's not a normal storm," Spike told me.

"What do you mean, it's not a *normal* storm?"

"I mean the storm is raging *within* the bounds of Mystic's End." Spike gestured toward the window above him. "It didn't come from anywhere, it isn't *going* anywhere. It's just here."

"How is that even possible?" I asked. I leaned over Gabe and looked up at the sky, squinting. "A storm can't just appear and disappear."

"What are you talking about?" Gabe leaned far back while I dragged myself across his lap. "Who are you talking to?"

"Spike. He said the storm's not normal."

"It's just a pop-up thunderstorm," Gabe disagreed. "It's the summer, we get those in the summer. They come, they rain, they disappear. It's not *that* out of character for this area, Fortuna."

"I didn't say it was out of character," Spike told

Gabe even though Gabe couldn't hear what he was saying. "I said it wasn't *normal*."

"We are here, sir," Jeeves announced, pulling into the parking lot outside the forest trail. "Unfortunately, I only have two umbrellas in the trunk."

"We'll be fine, Jeeves," Martin told him. "A little rain won't hurt us."

"Of course, sir."

We all climbed out of the limousine into the rain and scanned the parking lot in unison. There were few vehicles parked there. Just Martin's limousine, a tow truck, and an unmarked van.

"That's Lulu's tow truck," Gabe nodded and pointed. He heaved the heavy bag with the smoky quartz to his shoulder.

"Whose van is that?" Ollie asked.

"I don't know, but I don't see Pepper's car here," Gabe answered.

"The young woman's car has been found five blocks from where she pretended to break down, Detective Wilcox," Jeeves told him, looking up from scanning his tablet. "Members of our security team are searching the vehicle now."

"How do *you* know where she pretended to break down?" Gabe asked him.

Jeeves stared back and didn't answer.

"Members of your *security team* need to get

away from the car and call the police." Gabe stepped toward Jeeves. "You're going to wreck any evidence we might have of..." Gabe trailed off, unable to finish the sentence. "We need to process her car for evidence."

"Evidence of what?" I asked him. "What are we supposed to tell your boss, I had a psychic vision that something was wrong with Pepper? She hasn't been missing long enough for us to even file a missing person report. They have nothing to look *into*, Gabe."

The detective's face twisted in frustration as he searched for an argument to counter my point, but he couldn't find one.

"Gabe, she's right," Ollie told his friend, placing his hand on Gabe's shoulder. "I know you don't like this in between the lines stuff, but we are deep in it here. May as well go all the way, especially if it helps Pepper."

"Let me see that." Gabe reached out to grab the tablet from Martin's body man.

Jeeves jumped back with surprising speed and glared at the detective. "My apologies, Sir, but that will *not* happen."

Just then, my phone rang. I pulled it out and looked down, hoping it was Pepper. My jaw dropped when I saw the caller ID:

THE ROCK: ooo-ooo-oooo

"What the...Hello?" I answered.

"You need to get moving," a voice I didn't recognize told me.

"Who *is* this?"

"Tom Wilson," the voice on the phone told me as I started toward the forest.

"I don't believe you," I told the voice on the phone.

"Your red pajama bottoms have a hole above the knee," the man spoke rapidly. "Your greyhound snores like a freight train in the middle of the night. And I totally lied when I said I couldn't see outside the rock. You have a birthmark on your—"

"Okay, okay," I said, cutting him off and blushing. "So it's you. *How* are you doing this?" I led the group through the mud onto the trail.

"I don't know," he said. "As we got closer to this place, I felt stronger and stronger. Not quite so boxed in. Since I figured out how to manipulate the app better, it wasn't such a stretch to make a phone call. You have another app on your phone that hooks into your business landline. I used it to call your cell phone."

I put the phone on speaker so the others could hear.

"Are you remembering anything more now that you're feeling stronger, Tom?"

"Bill, Lulu, and I went out to dig rocks the night

I was killed," he said as we got closer and closer to the place Pepper and I found Tom's body. "I remember now. I told Lulu that night that I was getting back with Emily. She was pretty upset."

"Rick, her brother, says she's pregnant with your child, Tom. Obviously, she's gonna be upset," I told him. "Why on earth would you break up with your girlfriend on a rock hunting trip?"

"I don't know *anything* about Lulu being pregnant," Tom said hotly. "In fact, Lulu told me over and over during our relationship that she never wanted kids. We were *very* careful."

"This coming from a guy who may have gotten two women pregnant simultaneously?" Gabe muttered from behind me. "How careful could he have been?"

"I heard that!" Tom shouted.

"Of course you heard that. I'm carrying you on my back," Gabe countered.

The rain tapered off, and the sun's pale light was faintly visible through the treetops. Birds sang among the branches in the aftermath of the storm.

"Did you hear that?" Martin whispered, He held his hands out to stop me from walking. The group paused and listened.

"You just *can't* keep your nose out of other people's business, can you?" a gruff male voice with a southern drawl said somewhere off to the right.

"Steady," Jeeves whispered, crouching. "Whoever they are, they sound like they're only a hundred yards or so that way," The man pointed twice toward the voice with military-like precision. "We don't want some sharp-eared person to hear us coming."

It was more words in a row than I think I'd *ever* heard Jeeves say.

Spike rolled his eyes at Jeeves and floated quickly toward the voices.

"Thanks, Jeeves. I'm sure *none* of us could have come to that conclusion without you here," Gabe whispered fiercely at the man.

The phone was silent as we all listened.

"My business is other people's business, you *moron*," Pepper yelled loudly at the man. "You're not gonna get away with this, Bill Johnson! You're not going to get away with *any* of it!"

"No one's going to find you," he told her, and then he laughed menacingly. We all jumped as we heard three clangs. "In a few hours, you'll suffocate. No one digs here, so you'll never be found."

"*You* dug here," Pepper told him.

"No one will dig here now that a dead body turned up on this ground."

"It's mud now, you idiot," Pepper retorted. We all looked at one another and crept toward the voices. "How are you going to bury an oil drum in the mud with a small shovel? I mean, *really*? This is your big game plan?"

"The hole was dry this morning," Bill snapped.

"Well, the hole is filled with water this afternoon," Pepper said. "So, what's your plan B?"

"Shut up," Bill snapped again.

"Okay, so here's the deal," Spike said when he floated back. "Pepper is tied to a tree, but she's not harmed. It looks like someone might have hit her on the head because there's a little bit of blood on the side of her face. But at the *moment*, she's okay."

"Thank goodness," I sighed, though fear gripped me a moment later. Just because Pepper was okay now didn't mean she would stay that way.

"The guy Bill, he's a big guy, wearing overalls. Got gray hair and a shovel. From what I gathered, his plan is to stick Pepper in an oil drum and bury her. Problem is the hole he dug. It's filled with water."

"The drum would just float up if it's airtight," I gasped.

"Right, so he looks like he doesn't know what to do."

"Is Lulu there?"

"There's a woman there, but I don't know what this Lulu looks like, so I couldn't tell you if it's her," Spike said. "Honestly, she looks a little shell-shocked if you ask me. *If* she is a part of this, I don't think she's happy about it."

"Is she tied up or anything?"

"No."

I quickly whispered Spike's report to the others.

"Okay, who's armed?" Martin reached toward his ankle and pulled out a gun. Every man reached to various parts of their body and pulled out weapons of various sizes.

I stared, my jaw dropping. I was suddenly standing before four dangerous and lethal-looking men holding firearms at the ready.

"You knew you moved to the *South*, right?" Ollie whispered with a grin.

"Doesn't that mean *he'll* probably have a gun, too?"

"Won't matter." Gabe checked his weapon and loaded a bullet in the chamber. "One gun against four? Not a problem."

"Are we ready?" Jeeves asked.

"You stay here," Martin told me.

Fury bubbled up within me. I didn't care if this was the *South*, I didn't care if they were trying to protect me. I was tired of being treated like a helpless girl that needed to stand behind the big, protective man-posse.

I pulled my hands back and magically yanked every gun from every hand, disarming every one of the men facing me. Thrusting upward, I levitated all the arms five feet above their heads and stared each one of them down.

"You want to *rethink* that?" I whispered fiercely to Martin. I twirled my finger and made the guns dance in a circle as if they were rides on a merry-go-round.

The four men looked up above their heads, slack-jawed, and then slowly looked back at me.

"My apologies, I misspoke," he whispered slowly. "Would you *like* to stay here?"

"I would not, thanks for *asking*," I whispered back. I gently lowered the weapons. The men each grabbed the one in front of them, and then spent a few seconds passing them back and forth, getting the proper guns back to their original owners. "Everyone has their weapon back?"

"Yes, ma'am," Gabe told me respectfully.

I stepped in front of the group and gestured to Spike to lead the way.

The men followed me without protest.

* * *

I t was over in a matter of seconds.

Bill, his silvery hair and beard shining in the sunlight, turned in shock as we emerged into the clearing. Without a single word, I magically yanked the shovel from his hands and sent it flying safely behind him. With a quick downward thrust of my hand, I collapsed the oil drum into a flat metal disk.

My armed posse looked unnerved.

"Freeze!" Gabe pointed his weapon at Bill. With a sigh, the older man raised his hands above his head. "Get down on the ground!"

"But it's all *muddy*," he whined.

With a flick of my wrist, I sent him tumbling face-first into the wet ground. Another alarmed look from Martin, an amused one from Ollie.

Spike, meanwhile, was laughing uproariously.

"Are you okay?" I went to untie Pepper.

"Am *I* okay?" she asked in a taunting tone. "You're whipping your fidget fingers *all over this clearing*! Did you hit your head or something? You know everyone can *see* you, right?"

"We can talk about it later," I told her, tugging the last of the ropes free.

"How did you find me?"

"Magic," I whispered, and we hugged when she stood up. "I'm *so* glad you're okay. I was so worried."

"*Why* am I still in this stupid rock?" Tom shouted through the speaker on my phone. "I thought once you solved my murder, I was going to be able to get *out* of this thing?"

"Tom?" the woman sitting at the base of the tree

about twenty feet from us whispered, her eyes wide as her head swiveled wildly on her neck. "Tom? I can hear you! Tom?"

"Lulu Miller, did you hit me on the head with a rock?" Tom demanded.

"*What* in tarnation is going on here?" Bill asked, his face covered in mud. Gabe handcuffed him. "You have a recording of Tom?"

"This isn't a recording, you *idiot*," Tom spat. "Did *you* kill me?"

"Well, if that was *really* Tom, you would know, wouldn't you?" Bill said. Gabe secured a single handcuff to a tall, thick tree. "You were there, weren't you? No one else was!"

"Well, that kind of answers *that* question, doesn't it?" Pepper said.

"Obviously not." I pointed to the bag on the ground. "I don't see Tom, and he says he's still in the rock."

"I *am* still in the rock!" Tom shouted.

"Maybe we have to break it?" Ollie suggested.

"Where did you make that shovel fly off to?" Martin asked.

"Everyone just slow down," I said while Gabe helped Lulu to her feet. "We still don't know what happened, and I think until we do—all of what happened—Tom is going to be stuck."

"Let's hear it," Gabe said as he sat Lulu gently next to Bill.

"I'm not saying anything without my attorney," Bill told Gabe, trying to cross his arms.

"You don't have to say anything," Lulu whispered in a voice near to tears. "You told me what you did. You *told* me what you did." She turned to him, a look of rage on her face. "And I *hate* you for it."

TWENTY-ONE

"Look, I'll admit I was furious at Tom when he told me he was going back to Emily," Lulu told us as we gathered around to hear her tale. "I spent *two years* with the man making plans, and with one night, he undid *all* that." She took a deep breath and stared at us. "But I didn't kill him."

"I remember now!" the phone boomed. "You *were* there! You must have done it! You were furious at me for leaving you!"

"If I decided to kill you for screwing me over, Tom Wilson, I wouldn't have hit you from behind!" The puffy-faced tow truck driver glared daggers at the phone. "I would've come at you to your face! With a knife!"

"That's not exactly making us think you didn't kill him," Gabe pointed out.

"Yeah, well, I *didn't* kill him." Lulu crossed her arms. "Bill killed him."

"I did not!" Bill protested hotly. "The man fell. Tripped and fell. That's all it was, that's all that happened. I was there. I *saw* him fall."

"From your *house*?" I asked him. Bill glared at me.

"You saw him fall because *you* hit him on the head," Lulu snapped.

"The fact that you kidnapped Pepper and were going to bury her alive in an oil drum...I mean, that doesn't exactly make us think you didn't kill him, either," Gabe pointed out to the muddy man on the ground.

"Son, you need to figure out *who* you're accusin'." Bill squinted up at the detective. "Seems to me you don't know any more than you did walking into this forest today."

"I know you kidnapped my ex-girlfriend," Gabe pointed out. Pepper rolled her eyes.

"She looks fine to me," he shrugged. "She just wanted to come out here and go digging. You ain't got *nobody* that can say different."

"Hello?" Pepper glared at the man and waved. "You realize, since I'm not dead, I *can* still talk, right?"

"No one believes you anyway. You're the crazy tinfoil hat lady," Bill told her. "I'm an upstanding member of the Mystic's End Chamber of Commerce. I played golf with the mayor just last week. When's the last time any of *you* played golf with the mayor?"

"I bribed him last week," Martin told Bill. "Does that count?"

"Oh, please, you got your *own* secrets, Salvi," Bill sneered. "I ain't worried about you spillin' *mine*."

Martin's face remained impassive.

"We came here to hear Lulu's story," I interrupted the men. "Can all of you be quiet for just two minutes so she can finish?"

"*Sassy* little girl, aren't you?" Bill glanced at Martin. "Let's see how sassy you are when your *big bad boyfriend* isn't standing next to you."

My fingers twitched.

"I didn't kill Tom," Lulu repeated. "I couldn't very well kill somebody for cheating on me when *I* was cheating on them, you know?"

"*You* were cheating on Tom?" I asked her, surprised.

"I've never been a one-man kind of woman, not really, but Tom was as close as I ever came," Lulu sighed. "Even so, I think I always knew he would go back to Emily. He talked about her enough."

"I never said I would marry you," Tom told her through the phone.

"Did I say anything about *marriage*, moron?" Lulu snapped. "I swear, Tom Wilson, you think you're a lot more charming than you are. You *are* right about one thing, though. I did think our relationship was more important than it was to you. And I was furious when I realized it wasn't."

"What does this have to do with Tom's death?" I asked her.

"I was cheating on him with Bill," Lulu jabbed at the scruffy-haired man sitting next to her. "When I told Bill I was pregnant, he said it couldn't be his. Said he'd been snipped so he *couldn't* father a child."

"So the baby is Tom's?" Pepper asked, trying to keep up.

"That's what I thought the night Tom died," Lulu told her. "That's what Bill claimed. It wasn't until yesterday that Bill admitted he *lied*, and the baby could be his." Lulu blushed. "To tell you the truth, I don't have any idea whose kid this is."

"I'm still not following what this drama has to do with Tom's death," I told her.

"Bill slammed Tom in the head with a rock after I told about the baby." She cast her eyes toward the gray-haired man. "It wasn't a big rock, and Tom stumbled, but he was still conscious when I left the forest. I don't *think* it was an accident, but I think Bill just got mad at the way Tom was talking to me. When I left, Bill and Tom were still talking. Well, yelling. Maybe Tom *did* trip after that."

"Was it this rock?" Gabe pulled out the smoky quartz.

"No, it was *much* smaller," she said, shaking her head. "And it wasn't a crystal. It was just a regular rock."

"So, you hit him once with a small rock and then decided that worked so well that you'd hit him *again* with a bigger one?" I asked Bill, shocked. I knew Tom was standing when the fatal blow came down, even if he didn't realize it himself.

"I told you I ain't talking without my lawyer," Bill snapped back at me. "He tripped like she said."

"You killed him on purpose," I said.

"Yeah, well," Bill shrugged. "Sometimes, people just *need* killin'."

"That's *not* a thing," Gabe told Bill.

Bill shrugged again.

The murdering rock hound refused to say anything else about the confrontation he had with Tom in the forest. Tom, meanwhile, remained encased in the rock, struggling to recall the argument.

"Look, I don't know *what* happened after I left here," Lulu said. "But he didn't tell me he hit Tom and Tom fell down. I don't know why you killed Tom." She looked fiercely at Bill. "I was mad at him, sure, but he *didn't* deserve this."

* * *

"I think you have to go in for a deep dive," Pepper said as the five of us stood across from Tom's former lover and former friend. "He's not going to tell us, and Tom clearly can't leave the rock unless he knows."

"Tom, have you tried to leave?" I asked him.

"There is no visible door if that's what you mean," Tom smarted back.

"Spike, can you just go in there and help him out?"

Spike shrunk into a ball of light and dove toward the smoky quartz. He bounced off it the same way he would bounce off the walls when I first arrived in Mystic's End. Expanding again, he looked at me.

"That's a *big* nope," he said.

I looked across the clearing at Bill.

I had used magic to find Pepper, and since I had sensed she was in danger, I didn't feel particularly guilty about that. The nausea might have even been what Miss Bessie called a *shoulder-tap* from the universe to urge me to do it.

And I had *already* dug around in Bill's head. It wasn't like I was *deciding* to break another rule.

Right?

With an effortless dive, I plucked the information from Bill's head as quickly as I would pick a flower growing in a field.

It felt anti-climactic.

"He just wanted the mega-crystal," I shrugged. "Simple greed. I'm kind of disappointed, actually. He realized that since he would likely wind up with Lulu, *she* could make a claim for at least half of the crystal's proceeds if she was pregnant with Tom's baby. But first, he would try and get her all of it. Bill counted on Emily not knowing much about the find once Tom was dead, and no one knew yet they were back together."

With a flash of light, Tom exploded out of the smoky quartz and stood, glowing, next to Spike.

"That's it?" Tom asked me frowning. "He killed me for money? Days and days and days *in that stupid rock*, and you just had to find out that Bill slammed me in the head because he wanted my crystal? *Seriously?* You couldn't have done that deep psychic dive a few days ago?"

"Maybe if you'd lived your life a *little* bit more upstanding, Tom, it wouldn't have taken us so long to figure it out. And I don't think he *planned* to do it. He got upset with you because of the way you talked to Lulu, and decided the world would be better off without you in it."

"He's got a point, though," Pepper said. "We didn't figure it out."

"Just because I just plucked the reason out of Bill's head doesn't mean we didn't work out who did it on our own. The plucking was just the bow on top," I told her.

"That you could have done a few days ago!" Tom shouted angrily.

"No. I felt differently about doing that a few days ago," I told the ghost.

He glared at me, his jaw dropping.

"You're welcome, by the way," I told him pleasantly.

Another glare from the ghost.

"I'm going to see Emily," Tom huffed as he turned and walked down the trail. "Thanks for *nothing!*"

Spike and I gazed after him stomping away.

"You think he knows he can just poof there?" I asked Spike.

"Probably not, he's pretty new to this gig," Spike answered. "Should I go tell him? That's a really, *really* long walk, you know."

The two of us watched the ghost storm down the trail angrily, complaining loudly as he went.

"It *is* a long walk," I agreed and turned away from the ungrateful ghost and back to the clearing.

* * *

C hief Clutterbuck walked into the clearing, followed by Bobby Newsom and two tall, muscular police officers. "Why am I *not* surprised?" the chief asked accusingly as his gaze traveled over our group. "Do you have a name for this gang yet? Or can we give you one?"

"Chief, Bill Johnson murdered Tom Wilson." Gabe told his boss. He pointed to the sulking man handcuffed to the tree. "Lulu Miller can give a statement back at the station, but—"

"How did anyone murder *anyone* if I ruled the death an accident?" The sloppy coroner walked up to Gabe and the chief. "Tom Wilson's death was an *accident*. He tripped."

"Only he didn't," Ollie told him. "Hey, boss, nothing to be concerned about. Everyone gets it wrong once in a while."

"What are *you* doing here?" Chief Clutterbuck asked Martin.

"Fortuna and I are dating," he said.

"We most certainly are *not*," I disagreed hotly.

The chief looked back and forth between us

and then turned his suspicious eyes toward Pepper. "I don't even have to *ask* about you," he muttered.

"Hey, *I* was kidnapped! I didn't *choose* to come here. Though if it had been someone else they kidnapped, admittedly, I *probably* would have."

"Yeah, *sure* you were," the chief responded. He rolled his eyes and turned away from her. "You two, get those two." He pointed at Lulu and Bill. "Take them to the station. We'll sort this all out there."

Gabe watched as a young officer untethered Bill from the tree. The other officer gently helped Lulu up and began walking her toward the parking lot. Gabe followed the group until Clutterbuck barked out his name and pointed at him. "Not you. You're not going anywhere."

Gabe looked back surprised, nodded, and made his way back.

"I don't know *what* this is." The chief waved his hands. "But Bobby tells me you all seem to be turning up in the middle of things that you shouldn't be."

I sighed. "Look, Chief Clutterbuck, we tripped over a dead body—"

He cut me off. "Yeah, I'm not sure I believe that. I'm not sure I believe *you*," he said in an unfriendly tone. Looking back up at Gabe and Ollie, Chief Clutterbuck's eyes narrowed again. "As for the two of you, you're skating on *very* thin ice."

"Apologies, chief," Gabe told the man.

"I don't want apologies," he snapped. "I want the two of you to remember which side you're on."

"Which side would that be?" Pepper asked with some irritation.

Chief Clutterbuck gave her a withering stare.

"Stay out of police business from now on, Ms. Stanford. Ms. Delphi, I don't know *what* game you're playing, but I'm beginning not to like it."

He's beginning not to like it? This man hadn't had a kind word for me since the day I arrived in Mystic's End.

"You two?" Chief Clutterbuck said to Gabe and Ollie while Bobby Newsom stared silently from behind him. "If I keep finding you where you're not supposed to be, you're both going to find yourselves on suspension."

"Yes, sir," Gabe and Ollie responded.

"Let's go, Bobby," the chief muttered again and nodded at Martin. The two strolled away as if they had nowhere important to be.

"Well, at least he still likes *you*," I told Martin.

"Yeah, interesting, that," Gabe murmured, looking at Martin suspiciously.

TWENTY-TWO

"Gideon, sit *still*," I told the dog who posed on a pillow in the center of Mystic Memories Senior Living's multipurpose room. "They're trying to paint you. Try not to move."

Gideon sneezed.

"I wish we could have dogs," Harold Whatnow complained. He squinted at Gideon and dabbed paint on his canvas. "Tellin' a bunch of old people they can't have pets. It's a *travesty*, I tell you."

"At least they take us to the track once a week," Uncle Vito told the crotchety old man. "You can see dogs at the track."

"I don't want to look at dogs running in a circle

wearing a *uniform*," Harold snapped back at him. "I want one to sit next to me on the couch while I watch my stories."

"I still can't believe you watch that garbage," Uncle Vito told him.

"I got to see romance *somewhere*!" he barked back. "Not like *you* leave any of the ladies for the rest of us!"

"Why don't you try being a little friendlier, Harold?"

"Why don't you keep your trap *shut*!"

"Gentlemen, let's concentrate on the art, shall we?" I sighed. Miss Bessie snickered. She looked like she was about to say more when Rick Taylor walked into the room and waved me over. "We've only got about ten more minutes, folks. If you're not finished, I can bring Gideon back next week."

"Darn it, I should've painted slower," Harold grumbled.

"Is that even *possible*, slowpoke?" Karen Aston asked him.

"You shut your trap, woman."

"And he wonders why he can't get a date," Uncle Vito murmured loud enough for Harold to hear.

"Is there something I can help you with, Mr. Taylor?" I asked the nurse in a formal tone. Rick frowned at the distance he heard in my voice and looked down toward his shoes.

"I deserve that," he said, looking up and meeting my eyes.

"Deserve what, Mr. Taylor?" I asked him agreeably.

"Look, I'm genuinely sorry about unloading on you the other day," Rick told me quietly. He placed a light hand on my arm and steered me toward the corner. It was as far away from the old folks as he could get me without leaving the room altogether. "I wasn't myself."

"You know, when people are under stress? They become *more* like themselves, not less." He stared at me, his cheeks reddening. "I appreciate your apology, but you're right. I *didn't* deserve that."

"Can we start over?"

"Why would we do that?" I asked him. He looked startled.

"Maybe you won't believe me, but I *didn't* realize that Lulu was cheating on Tom. The whole situation with you and your friends?" He waved toward the window—as if my friends group was standing out on the sidewalk. "I *didn't* know the full story, and not knowing the full story...Look, I flew off the handle. Can't you just accept an apology?"

"I *did* accept your apology," I pointed out. "It doesn't mean I'm going to forget what happened."

Rick frowned and crossed his arms, clearly frustrated that his attempt at shoveling the pails of water under the bridge wasn't working.

The back of my neck prickled. Squinting, I suddenly realized this wasn't an apology with no other agenda.

He wanted something.

"What is it you want from me, Rick?"

"Who said I wanted anything?" he asked defensively.

"Well, you apologized, I accepted it, and you're still here." I held out my arms. "So? What is it?"

He looked concerned about my observation, his brows knitting together, and his eyes narrowing. "Are you trying to do that psychic garbage on me?" He practically spat *psychic* like it was a four-letter word.

"Rick, I need to get back to the class. If you have something to say, just *say* it."

"Fine," he uncrossed his hands and leaned forward. "Emily is still obsessed with trying to contact Tom. She's sitting in her house, crying, with a Ouija board. Because of what *you* said."

I frowned. That wasn't good.

"Just go to her and make up something about him moving on to whatever realm you think he goes to or wherever it is that he's gotta go to," Rick insisted. "You owe her that. The fact that she's all upset is *your* fault, anyway."

"You think it's my fault she's upset her husband was murdered," I said slowly. I stared him in the eye.

"I think it's your fault you're pretending to have some hotline into the great beyond, Fortuna. Everyone knows that what you used to do was bunk," he snapped, crossing his arms again. Leaning even further forward, he whispered, "Just because you didn't take money for it doesn't mean what you did to Emily wasn't a con."

"Leave me alone, Rick," I told him. As I turned, he grabbed my arm. "Hey!" I snapped, looking back at him. "Take your hands *off* me."

"I—"

Whatever Rick Taylor would have said was interrupted by a drooling, snarling greyhound thrusting his skinny body between us. Gideon's bared teeth were *perilously* close to the large nurse's...upper thighs. He must've realized this, too, because Rick dropped my arm and backed against the wall—his hands swiftly covering his junk.

I heard Uncle Vito chuckle behind me.

"I'll go visit Emily because I'm worried about her." Gideon continued to arch his back ominously.

"But you and I? We are *not* friends, and my visit has nothing to do with you," I told him coolly.

When I walked back to the other side of the room, Miss Bessie looked at me with a bemused smirk on her face. I raised my eyebrow at her, and she waved me over.

"You should've talked to me before you started sparkling all over town, dear," she whispered in my ear. "After you see Emily? Come back this afternoon and see me. We need to talk."

"We *always* need to talk, Miss Bessie," I told her.

"Yes, and we *never* do," she responded and then paused. "If we had? You would know that you need me to open that book."

"I opened the book," I lied.

"You shouldn't lie, dear, you're not very good at it," she whispered back and tapped my nose with her paintbrush. "Go see Emily and help the poor dear. Then come back and see me."

I nodded.

* * *

"Fortuna, you're here!" Emily shouted when she opened the door. Grabbing my arm, she dragged me into her home.

I was shocked to find Lulu Miller sitting on

Emily's couch. A Ouija board sat in front of her on the coffee table.

"Hello, Lulu," I nodded.

"You have to *stop* this!" Tom floated toward me, shouting while waving at the two women. "They're comparing notes! They're uncovering *every* lie I ever told them! And I can't make the stupid Ouija board say the things *I* want to say!"

"You're dead, and you *still* want to lie to these women?" I asked him out loud.

"You're talking to Tom!" Emily said. Turning to Lulu, she looked triumphant. "I *told* you she could talk to Tom! I *told* you!"

"Oh, I believed you. But after everything we found out about him, who would even *want* to?" Lulu leaned back and crossed her arms.

"There *must* be some explanation." Emily sat next to Lulu and grabbed her hand. "There must be!"

"Of course there is," the other woman told her. "He's a lying jerk."

I stared at the two women sitting next to one another, and it struck me how different they were. Emily was small and delicate, while Lulu was muscular and large-boned. Emily's expression was sad, while Lulu's was angry. Emily dressed in a sheer pink blouse with silky white slacks while

Lulu was in denim that *might* be older than she was.

"I have to admit, I'm a *little* surprised to find the two of you together," I said, sitting down in the chair to the right of the two women.

"My brother told me about Emily being pregnant, too," Lulu answered. "If this baby is Tom's, that means it'll have a brother or sister. I...I grew up without my family because my parents were cheaters." Lulu shifted uneasily. "No matter what happened between all of us, I *didn't* want that to happen to my child."

Emily nodded. "Lulu told me all about her situation. We don't want that for *our* children."

"I'm glad to see the two of you don't resent one another for what Tom did," I told them and glared at Tom. "Though *he* doesn't seem especially pleased about it, which is too bad."

Emily's face fell. "There's a lot about Tom I didn't know," she whispered.

"That we *both* didn't know," Lulu added.

"I can't believe he hid that big rock crystal from me," Emily said.

I frowned. "But it was in the newspaper."

"Well, I mean, I knew that he had *found* it, but he told me because of its size, and because he dug it up in the park, the state had confiscated it," she explained. "We were separated when he found it, and I guess he assumed we would get divorced. He didn't want me to have half of it, maybe?"

"You're kind of a jerk," I told the ghost.

"Well, I didn't know she was going to get *pregnant!*" he protested hotly.

"Yeah, see, the fact that you think *that's* the issue?" I pointed out to him and tilted my head. "That's kinda what makes you a jerk."

"I still loved him," Emily whispered as she lifted her head up.

"Me, too, but he's dead now," Lulu told her. "Which is probably for the best, because if I'd known all of this? I *probably* would've killed him myself."

"What are the two of you going to do now?" I asked them.

"Bill's signed over the rock shop to me," Lulu shrugged. "He knows he's going away for a long time, maybe forever. *If* this baby is his, he wanted it taken care of. Bill's not all bad. If it's *not* his," she winced a little bit. "Well, he felt it was the *least* he could do to make up for killing Tom."

"Since Lulu has the shop now, she's going to help me sell the mega-crystal," Emily smiled at her gratefully. "I don't know anything about their rock stuff, but she says that she can get an excellent price for it."

"I don't *want* to sell it!" Tom howled.

"You don't get a vote anymore," I told him. "You're dead."

Emily whispered, looking behind her in the direction I was speaking to. "Why is he still here? Doesn't he have to move on or something?"

"Some ghosts move on, some don't," I told her. "There's a bunch of different reasons Tom might still be here. Like making up for what he did when he was alive? Just a guess," I smiled at him. "Hopefully, he'll learn from the mistakes he made in his life as he watches the two of you be *much* better people than he chose to be."

"I have an extra bedroom," Emily nodded. "Lulu's going to move in, and we're going to help each other. So we don't have to be so alone."

Lulu nodded.

Not the ending I expected.

Judging from Tom's expression?

Not the ending *he* expected, either.

* * *

"Emily's actually pretty good," I told Miss Bessie when I entered her room. "Lulu and Emily are talking. Oddly enough, I think it worked out for both of them. Better than if Tom had lived."

"Well, that's a *terrible* thing to say," Miss Bessie said.

"Yeah, well, you didn't know Tom."

"I didn't ask you to come over here to talk about the dead mail carrier." Miss Bessie poked her bony finger into my knee. "Why didn't you tell me that you couldn't open the book?"

"How did you know I couldn't open the book I found?"

"Well, you didn't exactly *find* it, now, did you, Fortuna?" She examined me. Her expression was simultaneously amused and disappointed. "The town decided to *give* it to you, didn't it? But you can't open it."

"We *established* that. But how did *you* know?"

"Don't underestimate what *I* know, Fortuna," Miss Bessie warned me.

"Look, I would've come and talked to you more about the book, but when we were leaving the forest, we tripped over Tom Wilson," I explained, shifting uncomfortably beneath the weight of her stare. "He was trapped in smoky quartz, I *had* to get him out, and...well, I was just distracted, that's all."

"You take things in stride that would shock other witches to their core, young lady. I don't know whether to be impressed or worried."

"I've had a lot of practice not reacting to things, okay?" I told her defensively. "Maybe it's from how I grew up or going through all the things I did with the Magical Midway. I try not to get freaked out about things. Just deal with one thing at a time, step-by-step."

"When did you make the decision to start flashing your magic all over town?" Miss Bessie shot back. "That's a step that's as ill-advised as—"

"You know, you're not my high priestess—"

"Fortuna," Miss Bessie sighed and clicked her tongue. "I'm not trying to *control* you, dear. I'm trying to *help* you. Trying to *warn* you. This town... This town is special, Fortuna. There are things you need to consider before you begin flashing what you can do all over town."

"Like?"

"Like the fact that people who don't believe in magic will justify away *anything* they see," she told me wearily with a casual shrug. "If people don't believe in magic? They can see you levitate a house with their *own two eyes*, and they'll find a way to explain it to themselves so it makes sense to them. But there are more people in this town, Fortuna, that *believe*. And those are the people you have to worry about."

"There's *always* people that believe—"

"I don't think you are hearing me, dear," the old woman smiled at me. "They believe, and it won't be so easy for them to dismiss what they see."

"So?" I shrugged. "People see magic. What's the worst that can happen?"

"Gabe's mother," Miss Bessie said, her eyes shining with unshed tears. "Mary is the worst that can happen."

THANK YOU FOR READING!
I hope you enjoyed Sketchy Charms! Please think about leaving a review! Fortuna and Gideon's adventures continue in Book 4, The Art of Scrying!

KEEP UP WITH LEANNE LEEDS

Thanks so much for reading! I hope you liked it! Want to keep up with me?

Visit leanneleeds.com to:

Find all my books...

Sign up for my newsletter...

Like me on Facebook...

Follow me on Twitter...

Follow me on Instagram...

Thanks again for reading!

Leanne Leeds

FIND A TYPO? LET US KNOW!

Typos happen. It's sad, but true.

Though we go over the manuscript multiple times, have editors, have beta readers, and advance readers it's inevitable that determined typos and mistakes sometimes find their way into a published book.

Did you find one? If you did, think about reporting it on leanneleeds.com so we can get it corrected.